AWAKENED BY GRACE

USA TODAY BESTSELLING AUTHOR
ALICIA RADES

Published by Crystallite Publishing.
Produced in the United States of America.
Edited by Megan Linski.
Proofread by Emerald Barnes.
Cover design by Rebecca Frank.

To my fans who've stuck with me through the entire series.

1

I thought I could learn to live with killing the demons. Marek kept telling me that's what it meant to be a Davina. More than anything, I wanted to be a Davina. But I didn't want to be a killer.

And that's exactly what I was. A killer.

A murderer.

I sat alone on the cold concrete steps in front of Eagle Valley High School and stared across the full parking lot. Dense fog and silence filled the air, as if the town itself was mourning with the rest of us. I'd just abandoned my friends inside the gymnasium, which was the only place in town big enough to hold the memorial service for the Davina we'd lost three nights ago.

I crossed my arms to ward off the chill in the air. A heavy weight settled on my chest, but my stomach felt empty. I couldn't remember the last time I ate. I didn't feel hungry. I didn't feel much of anything. Only cold, empty, and broken. I wasn't sure how I was going to piece myself together after what I'd done.

A flash of purple entered my memory. I saw Trenton's face—the moment of shock that hit right before his heart gave out. Right before I stopped it. On *purpose.*

Trenton. My friend. A person I truly cared about.

A *person.*

Demons. Angels. Aedes. Davina. The labels meant nothing. We were all *people.*

Footsteps approached. I knew without looking that it was Marek. He didn't say anything as he lowered himself to the step beside me. Although he was only inches away, it felt as if a ghost of Trenton's essence lay between us, turning those few inches into an expansive ocean.

"Are you okay?" Marek asked softly, yet his voice still sounded too loud.

My gaze dropped to my feet. This was the part where I was supposed to tell him I was fine. But I couldn't lie, especially to Marek.

"Ryn," Marek pressed, like he thought I hadn't heard him.

He reached out and took my hand. I didn't pull away, but I didn't entwine my fingers in his, either.

I closed my eyes and took a deep breath. "I'm… alive." At least there was that. "What about you, Marek? Are you okay?"

He stared out into the fog, contemplating the question.

"It's a hard question, isn't it?" I asked flatly.

He nodded. "I've heard so much about this demon war. I've spent the last three years preparing to fight in it. But now that it's actually happening to me—to *us*—it doesn't feel real."

"I know what you mean," I whispered.

A beat passed before Marek spoke again.

"Why'd you walk out of the memorial service?" he asked curiously.

I shook my head. I didn't want to talk about it, but the words escaped my lips anyway. "I couldn't listen to them lie. The people we lost deserve better than that."

The whole town believed the deaths occurred in an accident at the community center. They thought Galen High students, parents, and staff were there for a fundraiser meeting. The Davina told them the building had a leaky section of roof that was never inspected properly, that it'd taken on too much water damage over the years and collapsed, killing dozens. The Davina even staged the whole thing while the town slept. They'd closed the streets surrounding the community center to keep people away from the demolished building.

The Davina Council had come into town under the guise of law enforcement personnel to conduct an "official investigation." In other words, they came to cover up the massacre.

"Why can't we just be honest?" My voice came out smaller than I intended.

Marek's lips turned down. "There are a lot of reasons the Davina keep secrets."

I'd heard every excuse in the book. Exposing ourselves would lead to mass panic. We'd be captured and studied by scientists. Keeping our secret was the safest way to protect the Originals, to protect Grace.

And still, I felt like the people of Eagle Valley deserved the truth. They *knew* the Davina we'd lost. They'd been business owners, cops, waiters, hairdressers, librarians, politicians… The list went on. Humans and Davina didn't live separate lives here in Eagle Valley. They were *friends*. Even those who didn't know the secrets of the Davina felt the loss and the sorrow.

"Do you want to talk about it?" Marek asked. "I mean, about him."

Him. That one simple word was enough to make my guts feel as if they were trying to force their way up my throat. I swallowed hard to keep the lump at bay.

"I'm sorry I couldn't fight harder," Marek whispered. "I'm sorry I couldn't prevent what happened."

I didn't regret saving Marek's life. I only regretted that I had to kill Trenton to do it.

The damn Power of Grace. That's all it was good for. Killing. So far, I hadn't seen it accomplish anything else.

"I thought I was meant for something greater than this, Marek," I said. "I mean, Grace must've chose me for a reason."

Marek shifted to drape his arm around me. It was hard to feel comforted in the wake of everything that happened.

"I'm sure she *did* choose you for a reason," he assured me.

His words hung in the air. I didn't care to discuss it any further, and Marek didn't push it. We sat in silence until the front doors banged open and people began flooding out of the school. Marek and I stood. I watched as faces passed—familiar and unfamiliar. Most people kept quiet, with their gazes locked on their feet as they headed to their vehicles. I finally caught sight of Allie and Kyle as they exited the building at the back of the crowd.

"Hey," Allie said somberly when they reached us.

"How are you doing?" Kyle asked me.

People needed to stop asking questions I didn't want to answer.

I sighed. "I don't know what to do anymore."

Allie stepped forward to wrap me in a hug. "You can't give up. Not when we're this close."

I shook my head. "I'm not giving up. I'm…" What *was* I doing? I certainly didn't feel hopeful. Was that the same thing as giving up?

Allie drew away from me. "I know how hard this is, but there's still work that needs to be done. We need to awaken Grace now more than ever."

My stomach sank. I didn't think I was ready for this. I wasn't sure I'd *ever* be ready for this. I'd managed to put it off while everyone grieved, but I'd promised to wake her as soon as the memorial service ended.

Allie noticed my fallen face. "What is it?"

I bit the inside of my lower lip. I wanted honesty, which meant I had to open up to my friends. "I don't want to use the Power of Grace again."

"It's just one last time." For once, Kyle was trying to be reassuring.

"Yeah," Allie agreed. "Once you wake Grace, you don't

have to worry about her power anymore. Grace will be able to end all of this. Things will go back to normal."

It was a relief to think about, but Allie was wrong. Things would never go back to normal. Maybe it'd be *her* normal, but *my* normal set sail a long time ago.

"Look." Allie gestured to the people quietly climbing into their cars. "These people need hope. Grace can bring them that."

I continued to chew on my lip without replying.

"We can wait until you're ready," Marek offered, but I knew he didn't mean it. None of us could afford to wait any longer.

"No," I said. "I think you're right. It's time to wake Grace."

2

My legs felt like noodles as they carried me back to my house. The silence between my friends was agonizing. I half expected someone to speak up and explain to me how this had all been an elaborate prank, but no one did.

I took a deep breath and descended the flight of stairs to my basement. The sound of my friends' footsteps behind me should've been comforting, but it only made me more nervous. It felt like I should be doing this alone.

I stopped in front of the Davina carving I'd found weeks ago. I could hardly believe the moment had finally come. All that stood between me and my destiny was a wall. My heart pounded so loudly in my ears that if any of my friends said anything, I wouldn't have heard them. My mouth grew dry, and my fingers quivered.

"What's wrong?" Allie asked softly.

"Ryn." Marek reached out and placed a hand on my shoulder.

I cleared my throat. "I just—what if…"

How did I tell them I was freaking terrified that something might go wrong? What if Grace wasn't here like we thought? What if I couldn't wake her like I was supposed to?

You won't know unless you try, I told myself.

I shook my head. "Never mind."

Somehow, I managed to steady my shaking fingers long enough to pull Meg's key out of my pocket and slip it into the lock beneath the Davina carving. I closed my eyes and twisted.

A horrible noise like crunching gravel filled the basement, and a large puff of dust exploded around me. I took a step back, coughing. Everyone else lifted their hands to shield their faces from the dust cloud. When I opened my eyes, I noticed a seam that followed the outline of stones. A section of wall had popped inward to reveal a door.

When no one made a move, I realized they were waiting for me. I stepped forward and pressed my palms to the cold, hard stone. The door swung open under my weight. The overhead light behind me illuminated a small section of dusty floor. Beyond that, I found nothing but darkness.

I reached for my phone in my back pocket, but before I could use it to brighten my way, a light shone from behind me. Marek had pulled a flashlight from the shelf nearby and handed it to me.

"Thanks," I said before turning back to the room.

The room was barely bigger than my bathroom. The

light from my flashlight reached the back wall. A large rectangular stone took up most of the space.

I inched my way inside and circled around the stone, keeping the flashlight fixed on it. A large carving of the same Davina woman that we'd found outside the door had been etched into the top. Instead of her hands at her sides, however, the woman held her hands together at her heart. A crack ran between them, like that part of the stone had deteriorated over the last century and a half.

She's here! She's really here! Excitement fluttered in my chest, and my worry melted away.

I barely noticed everyone else filter into the room. Allie and Kyle stood on my left while Marek stopped on my right.

Allie ran her fingers over the top of the stone. "It's a tomb."

Marek pressed his hands up against the decorative lip that ran along the perimeter of the concrete grave. "Let's open it."

I quickly slipped the flashlight under my arm and mimicked his stance. Allie and Kyle joined in.

"On three," I instructed. "One... two... three."

I pressed my feet to the floor and put all my strength into lifting the stone, but the top of the grave didn't budge. Everyone seemed to realize at the same time that our efforts were useless. We all stepped back.

There goes my excitement. We're going to need a freaking jackhammer to get through to her.

"Maybe it opens somewhere else," Allie suggested. "Like on the sides."

I shined the flashlight on the side of the smooth stone and found nothing. Everyone pulled out their phones and used them as lights to inspect the area they were closest to. I quickly rounded to my right and squeezed past Marek to see if there was anything. There wasn't.

I passed by Kyle, who was crouched near the door in search of clues. Past him, I found only smooth stone on Allie's side. I returned to my spot at the head of the grave and ran my fingers over the wings carved into the top.

My jaw tightened. How were we going to get to her? "Maybe we need to use the key again."

"Where would it go?" Marek asked.

"I don't know," I answered. "Kyle, can you grab the key out of the door?"

He hadn't stood from where he crouched. "Um… you should come see this."

I pressed my body to the cold wall to pass by Marek again. "What is it?"

Kyle moved out of the way so I could make out what he was looking at. I was vaguely aware of Allie and Marek squeezing in behind me to get a good look.

I shined the flashlight on the words carved at the foot of Grace's tomb.

Here lies Grace, a Davina of old.
The time will come when legends unfold,
When Grace will walk the earth once more,
Protecting from a demon's war.
To awaken her, you'll need a key,
An ancient object old as she.

Be wary; take not this task so light.
When Grace awakes, prepare to fight.

Kyle broke the silence. "A key as old as Grace? It can't mean Meg's key. Grace is thousands of years older than this tomb."

I didn't take my eyes off the words as I read them through a second time.

"Is it talking about the Power of Grace?" Allie theorized.

I shook my head. "I don't think so. It says *object*."

Kyle sighed. "We have to find *another* key?"

I shook my head, but Marek spoke before I could.

"*An ancient object as old as she*," Marek emphasized.

I pulled myself up from the floor. "Good thing we already have one of those."

Realization crossed Allie's face as I held my hand out to Kyle.

"Ooh." Kyle pulled the Davina Blade from the sheath hidden beneath his jeans. I traded him my flashlight for the blade.

I rounded back toward the head of the tomb. "There must be a lock built to the blade's unique shape."

Allie glanced around in search of a keyhole, and Kyle followed the blade with his light. My gaze flickered between the Davina carving and the blade. It was clear to me what I had to do. I placed the tip of the blade in the crevice between the palms of the Davina carving, hovering it just above where her heart would be. Then I plunged the blade into the stone.

A satisfying click filled the otherwise quiet room.

Allie gasped. "A perfect fit."

I removed the blade and handed it to Marek. Everyone returned to where they'd stood before and placed their hands on the tomb. With a large heave, we managed to slide the heavy stone aside.

"Quick, the flashlight." I eagerly held my hand out to Kyle.

I inhaled an audible breath when I saw what was hidden inside. A beautiful woman with skin dark as night lay motionless beneath me. Tight black curls framed her flawless face, and she wore a long white dress. Her hands lay folded over her heart. She looked as if she might simply be sleeping, but she didn't breathe. My heart hammered so hard I thought perhaps the sound of it might wake her.

"She's so pretty," Allie whispered.

Marek and Kyle drew their heads closer to get a better look. It was a long time before anyone spoke.

"How does this work?" Kyle asked.

I blinked several times, still mesmerized by the sight of the Davina in front of me. I'd heard so much about her, and here she finally was—in the flesh. I wasn't sure I ever truly believed we'd make it this far.

"Ryn?" Marek spoke my name with a hint of curiosity.

"Sorry, I just…" I didn't look up. Instead, I shoved the flashlight back in his direction.

"You have the Power of Grace. Shouldn't you—?" Marek started.

"I know what to do," I stated confidently.

I didn't know how I knew, but in the same way Grace's power led me to Eagle Valley, it told me how to awaken her. I lowered my hand into the stone casket and placed it upon hers—directly over her heart. Inhaling a deep breath, I relaxed to let Grace's magic flow through me.

A deep purple glow traveled down my arm, continuing from my hand to hers. Color returned to her body, leaving her dark ringlets shinier and her skin more vibrant. It was like watching something from a movie. An intense electric current filled me as I pulled more and more of Grace's power from the earth and returned it to her body, restoring their connection.

The intensity quickly dissipated as the last remaining threads of Grace's essence left my body into hers. It felt strange. I'd become so used to feeling that electric energy inside of me that it felt like something was physically missing. It was also a relief, like I'd gotten rid of a tumor, a burden I never wanted in the first place.

Grace's eyes sprang open, and she drew her first breath. I jumped away, stunned by her sudden awakening. Grace looked shocked at first, but after blinking her purple eyes several times, she seemed to finally focus on the faces above her.

My friends stared at her in awe. I didn't know if I should be impressed or freaked out.

Grace pushed herself to a sitting position.

Freaked out, I decided. It was like watching a zombie rise from the grave, only without the dead flesh hanging off her bones.

Grace turned until her gaze landed upon me. "Kathryn?"

I stepped forward. "I'm Ryn—Kathryn." I didn't sound particularly confident.

Grace reached out toward me. I wasn't sure what she wanted, but I gave her my hand. She took it and squeezed it lightly. Everything about the gesture felt cold.

"I knew you had what it took," she said.

I returned an uncertain smile. "Thanks."

Grace looked around the small, dark room again. "It's quite cramped in here, isn't it? Should we go somewhere more comfortable?"

I couldn't believe how casual she was being. This lady had been asleep for millennia and was talking to us like we were old friends. Except, I didn't feel like I knew her at all. I expected a smiling, happy goddess, but Grace seemed… different. Maybe that was what happened when you spent thousands of years in a deep slumber.

Marek rushed to Grace's side and helped her out of her tomb. We filed out the room, still in a complete state of shock.

In the main area of the basement, Grace stopped and closed her eyes. "Just a minute."

I recognized the concentration in her expression and the way she flexed her shoulders. Two large white wings rose up from behind her. She took advantage of the space and spread her wings as far as they could go. Though hers were much bigger than mine, the white feathers shined a similar purple.

Allie inhaled an audible breath. I half expected her to drop to her knees and bow down before Grace.

Grace opened her eyes. "That's much better."

Allie managed to pick her jaw up from the floor, but her eyes remained fixed on Grace. "Can I just say what an *honor* it is to meet you?"

Grace smiled like she agreed her very presence was an honor.

"Um..." Kyle said, like he wasn't sure he was allowed to speak. "I'm just curious... Maybe this is a stupid question, but how do you know English?"

"There are no stupid questions," Grace said. "Though my body has been resting for a long time, my essence and consciousness have been part of the earth for just as long. I have been watching, observing the world I was meant to protect."

"So you're aware of what's been happening?" I asked. "You know what happened here in Eagle Valley?" I wondered if she knew how many people her powers had killed or if that responsibility fell on me. I wasn't sure I wanted the answer, so I didn't bring it up.

"Yes," Grace said. "I'd like to start making preparations to retaliate right away. But first, I'd like to visit the injured."

Grace's suggestion sounded noble, but there was something about her that rubbed me the wrong way. I couldn't explain why, but I just had a bad feeling about her. Perhaps it was her eagerness to fight, or maybe it was the smug smile on her face.

All I knew was, I wasn't sure I'd awakened the goddess everyone was expecting.

3

The dense layer of fog from earlier hadn't lifted when we stepped outside several minutes later. Grace insisted she needed to spread her wings, so we took flight and led her to Galen High. It wasn't far, but I still worried we'd be seen.

Though Grace had been observing all this time, it was like she couldn't believe it was all real. She seemed intrigued by one of the neighbor's dogs, and she couldn't take her eyes off a car driving along the street below us.

"We're here!" Allie exclaimed when we landed in front of Galen High. Her gaze flickered toward the mansion, like she expected people to start rushing out to give Grace the red carpet treatment.

I stared at the back of Grace's head as we walked toward the doors. I wasn't sure what I was supposed to do at this point. Should I be kissing the ground she walked on? Racing out of Eagle Valley now that my part was done?

Marek paused at the front door. "Grace, welcome to Galen High School."

He twisted the doorknob and pushed the door open before stepping aside for Grace.

All conversation died. A small group of a dozen people were gathered around the fireplace in the common room. I recognized Fletcher and Casey's dad—Mr. Harris—among the group. The others were complete strangers, who I figured were part of the Davina Council. Most of them wore suits, like we'd just stepped into a business meeting for a big corporation. The usual scent of lemon cleaner was masked by the distinct smell of shoe polish and arrogance.

All eyes turned toward Grace. She didn't need an introduction; they'd been expecting her. Her white dress, flawless skin, and purple eyes gave her away.

The front door clicked shut behind us, startling me.

A guy with white hair and a bald patch was the first to compose himself. He fell to one knee and bowed his head. "Grace," he said in a breathy voice.

Several others moved to bow as well, but Grace raised a hand to stop them.

"That's really not necessary," she objected, but a smile spread across her face, like she gladly welcomed the gesture.

A tall guy with short black hair rose from a bow and stepped forward. He held his head high. If I had to guess, I'd say this guy was in charge.

"Grace." He reached out to shake her hand. "I apologize that we couldn't arrange a better introduction. We didn't expect you awake just yet. I'm Anthony Lucas, head of the Davina Council. Welcome."

I didn't like the way he said *welcome* as if he owned the mansion. This guy had probably never even been here before.

Anthony glanced between Allie and me. "One of you is Kathryn, I presume?"

I took a step forward. "You can call me Ryn."

He looked down at me past his nose. I read judgement in his eyes, like he couldn't believe *I* was the one who woke Grace. Or maybe he was just pissed he'd missed it.

Anthony stuck his hand out in my direction. "I've heard a lot about you. We planned to meet you as soon as possible, but I only just arrived."

Just in time to miss the memorial service, I thought.

Anthony's handshake lasted only a moment before he dropped my hand and turned back to Grace. "Can we get you anything?"

"I'd like to see the injured." She spoke with confidence, like she knew no one would refuse anything she asked.

"Of course, of course," Anthony agreed. "This way."

He led Grace to the staircase on our left. Conversation broke out again, and the other councilmembers quickly followed. My friends and I were pushed to the back of the group, like we were a mere afterthought.

Ever since I learned what I was, it was all about finding and awakening Grace. Now that she was here, I didn't have a clue what to expect. I didn't know where I fit in to all this anymore.

"Everything went well, then?" Fletcher asked as we ascended the stairs.

"Yeah," I answered. "Just great."

Except, it didn't *feel* great. I should've been jumping in excitement and shouting for joy, just like the rest of them. Instead, I felt like I was only going through the motions, but no one told me what the next move was.

We climbed the stairs to the third level. A set of double doors opened to a vast room with a slanted ceiling and hardwood floors. The sounds of chatter and the occasional groan of pain spilled out into the hallway.

We entered a makeshift hospital, a refuge for the Davina who'd been severely injured in the recent battle. At least two dozen Davina lay on cots that lined the long room. Volunteers and family members sat at bedsides changing bandages or keeping the injured company. Not a single person smiled. Even the volunteers looked as if they were in pain just being in this room where sorrow leaked from the walls.

"Donations are still rolling in," Anthony explained to Grace. "We had to keep everyone here, or it would arise suspicion. We couldn't bring this many Davina to the hospital at once. We heal too fast. And, as you can see, some of the injuries are Davina-specific."

He gestured to a girl my age, who sat propped upright on a cot. Her wings were spread out behind her. One hung in a sling attached to one of the wooden frames we used to prop up foam targets. I remembered her from the battle. The broken bones in her wing had been set since then, but I still wasn't sure she'd fly again.

Beside her, a man struggled to push himself up so he could take a sip of water. Judging by the way he held onto his side, I guessed he had broken ribs. Beyond him lay a guy with a broken leg and a girl with a broken arm, both wrapped in casts. Across the room, a woman applied ointment to a large gash on a man's abdomen. It looked as if a demon had used one of our blades to slice his skin open. It'd been sown back together with at least two dozen stitches.

Grace stepped farther into the room and spun in a circle, taking it all in. Sorrow crossed her face, like she couldn't believe what she was seeing. Her enthusiasm from earlier had vanished, and her eyes glistened at the threat of tears.

Conversations slowly died out as more and more people noticed the noise in the room decreasing.

Grace's voice cut through the silence. She sounded more confident than she looked. "Please don't worry. I'm Grace, and I'm here to help."

Whispers broke out around the room.

Grace?

An Original?

I can't believe it.

For the first time, I saw someone smile. Allie had been right. These people needed hope, and Grace was their answer.

"Grace?" The girl with the hurt wing rose her voice.

Grace slowly approached her and knelt beside her cot.

"Is it really you?" the girl asked. She stared up into Grace's purple eyes.

"It is," Grace replied with a nod. She sounded kind, but her lips curled down at the corners. "How can I help you, child?"

The girl reached out toward Grace. When Grace didn't take her hand, she let it fall limply off the side of the cot. I glanced to Marek to see if he'd noticed Grace's cold greeting, but he only stared at her in wonder, just like everyone else.

Grace continued her way around the room, stopping at each bedside but not touching a single patient. It was like she was afraid their ailments were contagious.

My friends and I stood forgotten in the corner as Grace paraded around the room and soaked in the glory of her return. I thought about pointing out my observations, but Allie and Kyle spoke so highly of her that I knew I'd only offend them.

"Are you okay?" Marek asked me.

I forced my lips into a smile. "Grace is back. Why wouldn't I be okay?"

Marek slipped his fingers into mine. "You're being so quiet. I thought you'd be..."

"Be what?" I shrugged. "I don't know what to say, Marek. I'm not the hero anymore. Grace is."

"Does that bother you?" he asked.

"What?" I recoiled. The accusation felt like a slap to the face. "I'm not jealous of Grace, if that's what you mean."

I'm just not sure I like her.

I caught Fletcher's gaze from beside Marek. He quickly looked away, but I could tell he'd been listening.

I lowered my voice so only Marek could hear. "Don't you notice how she's being a bit… cold?"

"Cold?" Marek's eyes followed Grace.

"She won't touch anyone," I pointed out.

Marek shifted uncomfortably. "She's been asleep for a long time. She probably just needs some time to warm up to being around people again."

I frowned. Could that be why she rubbed me the wrong way? Or, maybe Marek was right, and I *was* jealous of her.

Another hour passed before Grace finished making her rounds. My friends hadn't made any suggestions to leave, so I stayed with them in our corner of the room. Eventually, the chatter returned to normal levels. It sounded happier and more upbeat than before.

Grace moved to the center of the room. Silence settled once again as all eyes turned to her.

"Thank you for allowing me to visit you today," she said. "It has been a great honor. I want you to know I will do everything in my power to ensure nothing like this ever happens again. You have my word."

Her words sounded calculated and stale to my ears.

She continued. "To the injured, you have nothing to worry about. All I want you to do is focus on getting well. To everyone else, please go home and get some rest. Spread the word that we'll meet back here at sunrise." Grace took a breath, then rose her voice. "Tomorrow, we will begin preparing for war!"

My stomach sank the same moment cheers broke out around me. Even my friends joined in on the clapping.

Marek was the only one to notice I remained quiet, but he didn't say anything.

I stayed silent even as my friends and I walked back home.

"I'm not going to get *any* sleep," Allie said.

"Me, either," Kyle agreed. "How does Grace expect us to rest after we just met her? I'm ready to start preparing for war tonight!"

My gut twisted. How could war *excite* him?

Relief washed over me when we reached my house and Allie and Kyle continued across the lawn toward hers. I didn't know how much longer I could listen to them talk about how great it would be to fight the demons again.

Marek walked me up my front steps. "I'm sorry this is so difficult for you. I know it's hard feeling hopeful after what happened the other night, but with Grace here, things are already turning around."

I wrung my hands together. "Are you sure?"

Marek placed a finger under my chin and forced my gaze up to his. "I'm certain. You don't have to worry anymore."

Marek's warm arms wrapped around me. I tried to relax into him, but the doubt in his voice made me uneasy. Or was I imagining his doubt, too?

It's my paranoia, I told myself.

It was the same paranoia that told me no matter how hard she tried to disguise it, Grace was hiding something from us. It was only just a matter of time before I figured out whether or not my fears were justified.

4

My heart pounded as a figure moved through the trees. Something about his footsteps sounded familiar—but dangerous.

"Ryn!" his voice called.

Guilt slammed into my gut.

"Trenton?" I stared out into the dark, dense forest in the direction his voice came from. "Trenton, please. Let me explain."

"There's nothing to explain," he growled.

I whirled around and slammed into his bare chest. Trenton towered six inches above me and was a solid wall of muscle. His long blond hair hung in front of his hostile eyes. A large scar the shape of lightning cut across his torso.

I took a cautious step back. "Please. I'm sorry I—"

"Sorry for what?" he spat.

My hands shook at my sides. I slowly distanced myself from him, but he followed.

"Sorry for breaking my heart? For choosing Marek over me? For killing me?"

My heel met the base of a tree. I pressed my back against it, cowering away from him.

He didn't give me a chance to answer. "You should be sorry —about it all. About never giving the Aedes a chance to explain! I thought you were special, but you're as bad as the rest of them."

A fireball with a dark center and red outline formed in his palm.

"I don't know what you mean!" I cried.

Trenton's dark essence was already speeding toward my chest. I didn't have a chance to get out of the way before the impact stole the air from my lungs.

I woke in a cold sweat. My sheets had been kicked to the foot of the bed, and my heart pounded in a quick rhythm. The street lamp outside my window cast a sliver of light across the room.

I closed my eyes and forced my breathing to slow. What had Trenton meant about giving the Aedes a chance to explain? Explain what?

"Bad dreams?" a deep voice asked.

A yelp escaped my lips. I instinctively grabbed the first thing my hands found and threw it at the intruder.

Because my *pillow* was totally going to save me during a home invasion.

The mystery man caught the pillow and stepped forward into the light. My muscles relaxed when I saw it was Marek.

"Are you insane?" I hissed, listening intently to make sure I hadn't woken my mom. "What are you doing here?"

Marek crossed the room and handed me my pillow. I sat up in bed and curled my legs under me so he could sit beside me. I wore sweatpants and a tank top, but Marek was still dressed in his normal attire—jeans, a t-shirt, and his leather jacket.

"I couldn't sleep," he said. "Turns out, it's really easy to climb onto your porch roof and into your bedroom. The window wasn't locked. You were practically inviting me inside."

I swatted at him. "Don't flatter yourself. I keep it unlocked for my other boyfriend."

Marek laughed quietly, and I smiled back. I realized it was the first time I'd smiled in days.

"I can leave if you don't want me here," he offered.

"No." I reached out for him before he could stand. "I want you to stay. It's just… I'm dead if my mom finds out."

Marek wrapped an arm around me and placed a gentle kiss on my forehead. "Then we'll have to make sure she doesn't find out."

His soft, warm lips left my skin. I ached to have them touch me again.

What was I thinking? He was in my bedroom in secret, and all I wanted was another kiss on the forehead? I could do anything I wanted with him right now.

"We can talk if you want," Marek suggested. "Or not. It's up to you."

That was it? He wanted to *talk*? What kind of guy was he?

A gentleman, I thought.

I snuggled into his chest and took a deep breath, inhaling the fresh scent of his t-shirt. I didn't know where to start. "I just keep thinking about the people we lost. I don't know what I'd do without you."

"I'm not going anywhere," he whispered into my hair. "I promise."

I frowned. "You can't promise that."

"I'll always be there in spirit," he said, like that was supposed to make me feel better. It only made me think of death. "How about this?"

Marek stood. He stripped off his leather jacket, then reached over his shoulder and grabbed his shirt. He pulled it up over his head and tossed it to the floor.

My heart hammered in excitement and fear. Maybe he wasn't a gentleman after all. I think I preferred his wild side.

Marek flexed his shoulders, and two massive wings rose from his back. He turned to his left wing and pinched a white feather between his fingers. He winced when he tugged on it and it broke free from his skin.

Marek stepped forward and handed me the delicate feather. "Now you'll always have a piece of me with you."

I stared down at it. For a brief moment, my heart felt full.

"Marek, I—"

He reached out and curled my fingers around the feather. "You don't have to say anything."

I pulled it to my chest and spoke softly. "Thank you."

My words weren't enough to show how much I truly

appreciated the gesture. I only wished I had a good place to keep it.

An idea suddenly struck me. I stood from the bed and summoned my wings, then plucked a feather out like he'd just done to his.

Marek smiled and held his hand out to accept his gift.

"Hold on." I turned and crossed over to my desk, where I dug in the bottom drawer for my jewelry-making kit. Once I found it, I sat in my desk chair and began twisting wire around the end of the feather.

Marek sat on my bed and eyed me through the darkness. "What are you doing?"

"I said hold on." I smiled while I worked.

Marek fidgeted as he waited, and I could tell the suspense was killing him. I quickened my pace, then turned to him when I finished. A necklace with my feather attached dangled from my hand. Marek reached out slowly and took it.

I undid the clasp on mine and secured his feather around my neck. "Now we'll always have a piece of each other close to our hearts."

Marek placed the necklace around his neck and slipped his t-shirt back on, hiding my feather beneath his shirt. "Thank you, Ryn. It's perfect."

Marek reached out and gestured for me to join him on the bed. I lowered myself to the pillow and curled up next to him. My muscles relaxed, helping me forget the horror of the past few days. Marek pulled the blankets up from the foot of the bed and draped them across us. His body was like a furnace—warm and comforting. His hot breath passed across the back of my neck, and his arm rested over me with our fingers entwined.

Beyond a gentle kiss on the back of my head, nothing happened. Part of me yearned for more, but another part was simply grateful he was here and that he cared. All I needed right now was someone I could count on.

I didn't want to face any more nightmares on my own.

I woke the next morning feeling more relaxed than I had in weeks. Marek's heavy arm draped over me and weighed me down. I managed to wiggle free of his embrace and climb out of bed without waking him. A yellow glow filled the room as the first signs of daylight touched the sky.

At my dresser, I gathered a change of clothes and then tiptoed out of the room to take a shower. I sped through washing my hair and shaving my legs. I was dried off and dressed within minutes.

I poked my head back into my room to see Marek's forearm covered his eyes while he slept. I quietly shut the door and turned down the hall to the stairs. I was surprised to find my mom in the kitchen, already starting on her coffee.

"You're up early," she said without turning from the coffee maker.

Shit. She knows.

"I have stuff to do today." I tried to sound as innocent as possible.

Mom finally looked at me. She brought her coffee mug to her lips and took a sip. "You mean Davina stuff?"

I grabbed a banana from the counter and began peeling it. "Yes."

Mom frowned like she always did when we talked about the Davina.

"Grace is awake," I stated flatly.

Mom took another sip of coffee but didn't say anything. We both knew it'd just turn into another screaming match and I'd run off and help the Davina anyway. It's not like she could keep me from going to school, even though I had no idea what school would be like now that Grace was back. Would classes be canceled?

I snatched up another banana and left the room before we started fighting again. Marek was awake when I made it back to my bedroom.

"It's not much, but I snagged you some breakfast." I handed him the banana. "If you don't want my mom to slit your throat, you'll have to sneak out the way you came."

Marek raised an eyebrow. "You think your mom can take me?"

"You'd be surprised what she's capable of when she's pissed. Besides, we're late." I glanced out the window to see the sun had risen.

"My bike's parked outside," Marek said. "I'll meet you downstairs."

Minutes later, I was climbing on the back of Marek's motorcycle, and we were headed to school.

Marek pulled into a full parking lot, but the walk up to

the school felt strangely quiet, which was weird because the weather was decent and first period hadn't started yet. When we entered the common room, my stomach sank. We were met by complete and utter silence.

Everyone was gone.

5

"Oh my god, Marek!" I glanced to the clock above the mantel and confirmed we were on time. Where was everyone? Had they rushed into battle without us?

Marek took my hand. "I'm sure everything is fine."

If everything was fine, where were Allie, Kyle, and Fletcher?

"Let's check upstairs," Marek suggested.

My knees shook as we ascended two flights of stairs to the makeshift hospital wing. Relief washed over me when a volunteer told us everyone else was in the valley.

Marek and I hurried down the trail near the back of the school. The morning air was chilly for just a tank top, but I knew it would get warmer as the day wore on.

When we broke out of the trees, the valley was full of Davina. There must've been hundreds. Grace stood in the middle of the swarm with her wings spread out in all their glory. Excited chatter reached us from where we stood at the top of the hill.

Marek's face lit up when he saw the crowd. "Finally, we're getting somewhere. Let's get down there before we miss anything."

Marek pulled off his jacket and t-shirt in a flash. He held onto them as wings grew from his back. I followed his lead, and together, we glided down to the base of the valley and landed at the back of the group.

Grace cleared her throat. The crowd responded by quieting and turning their full attention toward her.

"I think we're ready to get started." Grace projected her voice to the people in the back.

While she spoke, my eyes scanned the crowd. Davina of all ages had gathered to hear Grace speak. I even noticed Dylan, Ethan, and Logan, the freshmen in our mentor group.

It didn't seem right that they were here. They were too young.

My eyes landed on Allie and Kyle standing next to Fletcher and Allie's dad, Jay. I gestured to Marek, and we quietly made our way over to them. Allie smiled at me but quickly returned her eyes back to Grace.

"Our biggest advantage in fighting the Aedes is our numbers," Grace continued. "That is why I have decided to train Davina of all ages in battle tactics."

My stomach twisted uncomfortably. She wanted children to fight with us?

Nobody objected; they just stared at her in awe. I was stunned by their silence.

"I have recruited active Protectors to assist in this training." Grace gestured to a group of Davina behind her.

At least fifty young men and women held their heads high and stared straight ahead, looking like perfect soldiers. I shuddered to think that this was what Galen High was preparing me for.

I turned to Marek and kept my voice low. "I thought our people were already trained in this kind of thing."

Marek shifted his weight between his feet and nodded. "I'm sure it's just a refresher. Plus, Grace knows things we don't. She'll want to teach us."

"What about Ethan and them?" I argued. "They've hardly trained at all."

Marek didn't have an answer for me. He just bit the inside of his cheek and stared straight forward.

What the hell, people? Don't you care about your kids?

Where were the protesting parents? The ones demanding to call in more Protectors so their kids wouldn't have to fight?

I continued to eye the crowd while Grace spoke. Her instructions seemed like they were meant to inspire, but to me, they didn't sound authentic.

I wanted to slap the Davina and tell them to pull themselves together, to *think* for themselves. I couldn't believe no one was speaking up about throwing fourteen-year-old children into this war.

Chatter erupted around me following something Grace said that I missed.

Well, damn. I'd remained quiet for too long. If no one else was going to say something, I would.

"Shall we get started?" Grace asked the crowd.

"Hold on!" I shouted from the back.

All eyes turned toward me. I felt like a zoo animal on display.

I cleared my throat. "Shouldn't there be an age limit?"

Grace didn't have a chance to answer before Ethan spoke up.

"What does age matter?" he asked, clearly offended.

"Sorry, Ethan, but you haven't trained enough for this," I said sympathetically.

"Neither have you," he argued.

It felt like a slap to the face. He wasn't exactly wrong.

"Two weeks ago, you didn't want to become a Protector," I pointed out, trying to talk some sense into him. He'd even made it sound like his parents were skeptical. "Now you're going to race head-first into battle without any clue what you're doing?"

Heat rose to the surface of my skin, and I clenched my hands into fists. This wasn't right.

"That's what we're training for," Logan retorted from beside Ethan. "Grace is here now. We don't have any reason to be afraid."

The crowd murmured in agreement.

Grace rose a hand, and the Davina quieted. When her eyes fell on me, the crowd parted to create a path between us. I shifted uncomfortably under her stare.

"We can use as many Davina as we can get," Grace said. "I can't stop anyone who wants to fight. The best I can do is prepare them for what's to come."

"Do we even know what that is?" I asked.

People around me scoffed. Whispers broke out, and I swear I heard someone call me an idiot. For a brief moment, my eyes met Casey's. I was surprised when she shot me a sympathetic expression instead of joining in on the skeptical stares. I wasn't sure Casey was buying any of this shit either.

"We can discuss that as part of our practice," Grace said.

My shoulders fell when I realized there was no point in arguing with her. When Grace saw I had nothing more to say, she turned her attention back to the other Davina and began splitting them into training groups.

"Seriously?" I turned to my friends and kept my voice low. "No one has any problems with this?"

"Grace knows what she's doing," Allie said, defending her.

"Does she, though?" I asked.

Kyle frowned. "At least she's doing something and taking action."

"This isn't action!" I gestured to the Davina around me, who were still trying to decide which groups to break off into. "It's not even organized. It's chaotic."

"Be patient, Ryn," Marek encouraged. "Grace is only one person trying to guide all these Davina. Give her a chance."

I waited for Grace to share some sort of battle secrets or for something grand to happen, but it never came. As groups formed, all they did was conjure essence and spar each other. It was the same boring crap we'd been doing for weeks. The only useful thing I noticed was Mr. Harris demonstrating to a group of teens how to snap a demon's neck. My group listened to a Protector tell the story of his first kill. It was totally useless.

I couldn't sit around and watch this nonsense any longer. I abandoned my group. Marek's eyes followed me, but he didn't protest as I approached Grace.

"Grace, can I have a minute?" I asked.

Her eyes never met mine as she strolled from group to group, observing. "What is it?"

I took a breath. "I'm just wondering why we're wasting time doing all this while the Aedes are out there, probably gathering new recruits. Doesn't it make sense to strike right away while they're still weak? Or at least try to gather intel on their next move? Why are we practicing when most people here already know what they're doing?"

I noticed Casey in a group nearby watching me, listening. Her expression remained neutral. I couldn't read her.

Grace finally stopped and looked at me. "I'm not sure why you continue to question me like this. I'm doing what has to be done. Why can't you just trust me?"

That was a good question. Maybe it was because I didn't grow up with the stories of the Originals. Everyone else saw her as a goddess before they even met her. No one else was about to question her.

I bit my lower lip. If I started a fight right here in the midst of her loyal followers, they'd tear me to shreds—perhaps literally.

"Return to your group, Kathryn," Grace ordered. God, she sounded like my mother. "You need to be as prepared as everyone else, and frankly, you have a lot of catching up to do."

My teeth ground together.

Screw this. This whole thing was ridiculous.

I turned from her without another word. Back at my group, the guy was going on about his third kill. It sounded more like he was bragging than teaching, but Allie and Kyle were eating it up. Marek and the rest of them didn't notice me breeze past them and take flight. I didn't look back to see if Grace saw me, either.

I landed at the top of the hill and started down the trail back to the school. I wasn't sure where I was headed or what I was going to do at this point. All I knew was that I couldn't stand around and watch the circus Grace was running.

I decided to head up to the hospital wing and see if they needed any help there. Even if I was just keeping someone company, at least I'd be helping. I hurried up the concrete steps at the back of the school and reached out for the door handle.

Before I could twist the knob, a cold hand clamped around my mouth. My heart leapt inside my chest as my feet flew out from beneath me.

A moment later, an electric shock slammed into my back, and everything went dark.

6

Confusion clouded my mind. I was being carried. Or was I flying? Every so often, I caught a glimpse of color as my eyes peeked open. Then, that shock would hit my chest again, and I would lose consciousness.

My body dropped onto a hard surface with a *thud*. Strong hands propped me up. I hadn't gathered enough strength to peel my eyes open yet.

Slowly, the world came back into focus. I found myself in an unfamiliar room, lit only by the daylight seeping in through the curtains in the adjoining living room. A worn hardwood floor stretched out in front of me and met a door with a splintered frame. The living room split off in one direction from the entrance, while the kitchen sat on the other side. Stairs rose to a second level behind me. To my right, a small table below a cracked mirror had been knocked over. A vase lay shattered on the floor, but the flowers had withered away to almost nothing. A thin layer of dust coated everything. It didn't look like anyone had lived here for years.

Panic immediately set in when I noticed my hands were secured together behind me. I scrambled to get to my feet, but before I could, a foot connected with my gut, and I fell to the floor again.

"There's no point in struggling," a deep voice said.

My head snapped upward. A tall figure in a black cloak stood above me with his arms crossed over his chest. The room was too dark for me to see his face.

Fricking demons.

"You're too late," I snapped.

"Too late for what?" He sounded genuinely curious.

"Hurting me won't accomplish anything. Grace is already awake." Maybe that'd convince him to let me go. I doubted it.

The demon shook his head. "I don't want Grace. I want *you*."

"I don't have the Power of Grace anymore. I'm useless to you."

"No, you're not," he said in a cold voice.

"Then what *do* you want me for?" Fear didn't come across in my tone—only anger. I'd had enough of this demon shit to last me a decade.

The demon reached for his hood and lowered it before squatting to my level. I kept my eyes on his to show I wasn't afraid, but the truth was, his dark eyes and thin, pale features made me uneasy. Behind his angered expression, something about him looked familiar... and dangerous. Maybe that was just a demon thing.

"Allow me to introduce myself," he said. "I'm Malcolm. I believe you've met my son."

The air left my chest.

"You're Trenton's dad?" I didn't know why I said it like a question. The answer was obvious.

Malcolm's lips pressed together. "Rumor has it you killed my son."

"I didn't mean to!" I said desperately.

"*Didn't mean to?*" Malcolm threw my words back at me in disgust. "You don't kill people on accident!"

"He was trying to kill my friend!" I tried to justify.

"And you thought your friend's life was worth more than my son's?" Malcolm roared. His face came so close to mine that I had to turn away from him to keep our noses from touching.

My heart pounded, and my breath wavered. I spoke in a whisper. "I didn't want him to die. Please believe me."

Malcolm rose to his feet. "Believe you? You're a Davina! I don't *trust* Davina."

I couldn't keep the words from escaping my lips. "You trusted Trenton."

"Don't you talk about him like you knew him!" Malcolm shouted.

Pain shot across my cheek as his hand cracked against the side of my face.

"You think the Davina are all *high and mighty*. You're not! Every Davina I've ever met had to *take* something from me. First it was Sylvia—Trenton's mother. We were in love, you know. Apparently, she didn't love me enough to bear the thought of others knowing she had my child.

She ran away and took my heart with her. *Her* mother wasn't much better. She didn't want me around Trenton, but I didn't give her a choice."

While he spoke, my eyes scanned the house in search of an exit. I didn't feel the familiar weight of my phone in my back pocket, so I couldn't even entertain the idea of calling for help. The only exit I found was the front door. Even though the wood was splintered around the handle, and it was probably just hanging loosely from its hinges, I didn't think I could get it open while my hands were out of commission.

"When *she* died," Malcolm continued, "the Davina Council found out I'd been hanging around. They raided our house to get to me. Look at it. It's despicable." He glanced around the disheveled home.

"So this is where Trenton grew up?" I had to keep him talking to give myself a chance at escape. Not that I had much of a chance. I needed to figure out how to get untied first.

"It *was* our home," he spat. "Before the Davina destroyed it."

Davina wouldn't do that... would they?

"Killing me isn't going to help you get your revenge on the rest of them," I said. "They don't care about me now that Grace is back. It's not going to bring Trenton back, either. Believe me, if there was a way to bring him back, I'd do it myself."

Malcolm scoffed. "I told you before. I don't believe anything the Davina say. You don't trust us. Why should *we* trust *you*?"

"Why *would* we trust you?" I snapped. Was he actually suggesting demons were worth trusting? "You feed off human essence and play your stupid games with them."

My mind flickered to Clinton and the horrible things he'd done to my mom. Maybe there was a reason my friends wanted to rip the head off every demon they saw.

"We do what we need to do to *survive*," Malcolm snarled. "If that means borrowing a bit of essence, taking human lives, or killing Davina to protect ourselves, we'll do it."

What did he mean *to survive*? I thought the demons fed on human essence for fun—because they'd been oppressed for so long that it was the only way for them to feel they had any power. Was there more to it than that?

"What do you—?"

The air left my lungs as Malcolm's foot slammed into my stomach again.

"All I wanted was a life with my son, and you killed him!" he roared.

Malcolm kicked me again, sending me tumbling to my side. The right side of my face connected with the hardwood floor.

"Help!" I shrieked, hoping someone would hear me. "Help me!"

"No one's coming to your rescue," Malcolm taunted.

"Please," I begged. "Can't we—"

Malcolm shoved his fingers into my hair and wrenched my head upward. "Your time for begging is over. You think I'll give you a second chance when you didn't allow the same for my son?"

I couldn't hide the fear and desperation in my voice now. "I told you, I—ow!" I screamed as Malcolm slammed my face into the floor.

Malcolm's fist rushed toward my jaw, but I kicked my feet into the air to block him. My feet sank into his stomach, and he stumbled back. I used the split second I had to roll over and get to my knees. I wasn't on my feet before Malcolm's weight crashed into me. Without my hands free to catch myself, my forehead knocked into the wall. The room spun around me as I rose to my knees again.

"Please, Malcolm. You don't understand." I didn't know what else to do but beg.

"If you think putting on an innocent little girl act is going to spare your life, you're wrong," he growled. "It won't work on me."

While he spoke, I channeled essence into my palm. I wasn't sure what I was going to do with it, but it was the only option I had left.

Something was wrong. I felt the electricity run down my arm, but it didn't sizzle with the same charge I was used to. Had Malcolm's beating drained me that much?

It suddenly occurred to me that wasn't the case at all. I didn't have the Power of Grace anymore. My essence wasn't as strong. I was... *normal*. At least, normal for a Davina.

The realization distracted me. I didn't have time to duck out of the way of his next attack. Malcolm shoved me backward. My legs twisted under me, and I fell onto the stairs. The edges dug painfully into my spine. Malcolm stood above me with a dangerous look on his face.

"Why are you doing this?" I screamed. "Stop dragging it out and kill me already!" I didn't mean it. I didn't want to die.

Malcolm's nostrils flared. "That'd be too easy. I want you to *suffer*."

Malcolm could hurt me all he wanted. Maybe I even deserved it for what I'd done. But one way or another, I was going to make it out of here alive—even if it meant I came out broken.

I narrowed my eyes at him. "Bring. It. On."

Malcolm welcomed my challenge and bent over me. A moment later, my skin turned cold.

Malcolm's anger turned to curiosity. "I've never fed on Davina essence before. I'm not sure anyone has. It's different. Stronger."

Is that what the chill was? Was Malcolm stealing my essence?

Fear slowly fell to the back of my mind as a new emotion overcame me. It began as desperation, melting away the terror that consumed me. It left behind a strange, almost comforting feeling. This new sensation tingled its way through my body, offering me strength when I couldn't seem to find it myself.

What was this? It was almost like the Power of Grace had returned, but it was different. It was my own. Instead of pulsing through my body the way Grace's power did, it flowed smoothly.

I concentrated on my essence energy and pulled it back, resisting Malcolm's gross invasion. My muscles tensed, and heat returned to my skin as I tried to block him out.

Malcolm gritted his teeth. "There's no need to fight it."

"Please… stop…" I struggled to say. I could feel my essence being pulled away from me.

At the same time, that strange new power grew as my struggle for survival intensified. It suddenly occurred to me that maybe I could use it to my advantage.

This was my way out. I knew how I was going to survive. It didn't matter that my hands were tied. I'd killed five demons at once without my hands. Malcolm would never see it coming.

And so, I let my defenses fall. I freely let my essence flow from me to Malcolm. It was the only way I could access my essence myself. It was the only way I thought I might survive long enough to get out of this house. And I *had* to survive.

The channel opened between us again, and that strange tingle across my skin grew more prominent. The hairs on my arms stood. Instead of channeling my essence to my hands like usual, I brought the energy to my heart, holding back only slightly so it wouldn't be too much for my body to handle.

Before I could see what this new power was capable of, the front door burst open.

race stopped abruptly in the doorway to take in the scene. Several men in suits quickly filed in behind her. Malcolm took one look at the group and shot to his feet. He sprinted away, passing straight through the wall leading to the kitchen. The group of men who'd arrived with Grace immediately raced after him.

I noticed Fletcher in the group as he rushed to my side and knelt beside me.

"Ryn, are you okay?" His voice filled with worry.

I let out a breath of relief. "I am now."

Fletcher helped me sit up and began untying my wrists. I knew Malcolm had used fabric from a demon's cloak because I'd seen demons use the trick before. It was the only tool he had to bind me.

Grace took a slow step forward. "We're glad we found you before you were hurt."

That depended on her definition of *hurt*. The long stretch of black fabric fell from my wrists, freeing my hands. I lightly touched my swollen face. It was tender, but Malcolm hadn't broken skin.

My eyes turned toward Grace. She stood awkwardly, like she wasn't sure what to do.

"How'd you find me?" I asked.

Fletcher offered a hand to pull me to my feet. "Someone in the hospital wing saw you get taken. One of the volunteers flew after you but lost you. Another came to get us. Luckily, one of the councilmembers remembered this place from a few years ago. It was a hunch considering the direction the Aedes took you."

One of the guys returned, huffing. "We lost him, Grace."

"Don't worry," she said without looking at him. "We rescued Ryn, and that's what's important."

Her words sounded more like a formality and left a bad taste in my mouth. She shouldn't have been the one to save me. She should've let me save myself. At the very least, she should've let Marek come along. He was probably worried sick about me. And I didn't even have my phone to call him and tell him I was all right.

"Should we get back to the school?" Fletcher suggested. "There's a car waiting outside."

Fletcher led me through the front door. Trees surrounded the house on all sides, and a long gravel driveway stretched out to a quiet road. No wonder no one had heard me. We were in the middle of nowhere.

Two big black SUVs, no doubt courtesy of the Davina Council, sat parked in the driveway. Fletcher ushered me into the back seat of the first SUV.

Fletcher and Grace lectured me on the twenty-minute drive back to Eagle Valley.

"You shouldn't have wandered off," Grace scolded.

"I didn't!" I defended. "I was right outside the school."

"How many times have I told you to stay with someone else at all times?" Fletcher said.

I expected sympathy from Fletcher. Why was he treating me like this?

Because he's siding with Grace, I thought.

"Something happens to you every time you're alone," Fletcher pointed out.

I stared out the window at passing corn fields. "Yeah, I know."

Why were they acting like it was my fault I'd been abducted? Maybe they should be blaming themselves for not having decent security at the school. We were at war, after all.

I held my tongue.

Several minutes later, someone's ringtone cut through the silence. The councilmember who was driving answered his phone. He nodded his head along to the person on the other end of the line.

"Okay," he said. "We'll be there shortly." He hung up and turned to Grace, who sat in the passenger seat. "They found it."

She nodded once. "Good."

"Who found what?" I asked.

No one answered. It was like they hadn't even heard me.

We pulled up in front of Galen High several minutes later.

"Everyone else is still in the valley," Grace said to the driver. "We'll meet them there and let them know."

"Let who know what?" I asked Fletcher as we stepped out of the vehicle.

Fletcher led me in the direction of the valley. "You'll find out soon enough."

I huffed but followed him without another word. Why did it seem like the adults around me no longer wanted me to be a part of this war? It was like they'd only rescued me to keep their reputation intact.

When we arrived in the valley, the Davina were still split into groups. I wasn't sure they'd even realized anyone left to find me. I figured I was safe enough here, so I spread my wings and abandoned Fletcher at the top of the valley. I landed beside Allie and Kyle. They were taking lessons from Mr. Harris on the quickest ways to kill a demon using a Davina Blade. At least that lesson was useful.

Allie rushed over to me when she saw me. "Oh my god! Ryn…"

First things first. "Where's Marek?" I asked.

"Looking for you," Kyle said as he hastily followed behind Allie. "He headed up to the school, like, an hour ago. I thought he would've found you by now."

"Yeah, well—"

"Ryn!" The sound of Marek calling my name distracted me.

I turned to see him soar out of the sky and land in the

grass fifteen yards away. He pulled his wings into him and quickly closed the distance between us.

"Ryn, where have you been?" He gripped onto my shoulders, and his eyes danced across my face. Worry filled his expression. "I looked everywhere for you—up at the school, at your house… What happened to you?"

Long story. I guided his hands off my shoulders, hoping it'd show him I was all right and he could calm down.

All around us, Davina training slowed. The valley quieted as more and more eyes fell upon me. Whispers filled the training area.

"Shit." I nervously ran my fingers through my tangled hair. "Is it that bad?"

"Bad is an understatement," Allie said under her breath. Her eyes darted between the Davina who'd stopped to stare. "Ryn, you have two black eyes and blood under your nose."

I swiped my finger across my upper lip. A small amount of dry, crusted blood flaked off.

"What are you looking at?" Kyle snapped at the closest group. "You should be training."

A couple of guys from my physical combat class scoffed and rolled their eyes. Davina returned to their practice, but I could still sense eyes on the back of my head.

"I was going to help the volunteers in the hospital wing," I started in a low voice so only my friends could hear. "But then…"

"Then what?" Marek's expression hardened.

I resisted the urge to roll my eyes. "What happens to me every time I'm alone?"

Kyle inhaled an audible breath. "You were attacked? *Again?*"

I crossed my arms. "Kidnapped is more like it."

Allie's brows drew together, and disbelief crossed her face. "You're serious?"

"I'm serious," I deadpanned.

Marek leaned in closer to inspect my injuries.

Allie's expression fell. "You were attacked with all these Davina here? Or *was* it a Davina?"

"It was a demon," I said. "He must've been watching for me."

A muscle popped in Marek's jaw when he drew away from me. "What'd the bastard do to you?"

I gave them the condensed explanation.

Marek's fists tightened. "I'm gonna kill—"

"No," I stopped him. "He's gone for now. I'm fine."

"And he'll be back," Marek growled.

"I can protect myself if he gets close to me again," I stated confidently.

"How?" Kyle's voice filled with concern and skepticism. "I mean, you don't have Grace's power anymore, do you?"

"No," I answered, "but I think I have something similar."

My friends leaned in curiously, and I told them about the strange power I'd felt earlier.

"I think I might be different than other Davina," I admitted. God, I sounded full of myself, but it was the only explanation. "Maybe it's why Grace chose me in the first place."

"Can you show us?" Allie asked.

I glanced around at the Davina around us, but no one

was watching. I held my hand out in the middle of our small huddle. I concentrated on that strange energy I'd felt earlier, but I couldn't find it. All that glowed in my hand was a normal white orb.

"Maybe it doesn't work unless I'm in danger," I theorized. "Kind of like how the Power of Grace didn't work for me at first unless I was protecting someone."

"Davina," Grace called from where she stood at the center of the valley.

My friends and I turned our attention toward her, as did everyone else. She gestured for the group to come in closer so everyone could hear.

"We can talk more about this later," I whispered under my breath.

"I have great news!" Grace said with a gleeful smile. "We've found an Aedes camp outside of town."

Several people gasped.

"These are the Aedes who recently led the attack on Eagle Valley," Grace continued. "I believe they are gathering more Aedes to launch another strike on your town. We must stop them before they have the chance."

"Yeah!" someone shouted in agreement.

"That's why tomorrow, we—the Davina—will attack first." Grace sounded optimistic. "Anyone who is able to fight is expected to arrive here at sunrise. We will continue to train today so that we can go into battle tomorrow prepared. Everyone will have a chance to rest. And then tomorrow, we will win this war!"

The crowd erupted into cheers. Allie jumped up and down excitedly, and Kyle shot his fist into the air. Marek glanced between me and Grace, like he didn't know whether to join in or not.

I didn't like this. Did Grace really think a single day of training would prepare us for battle? I knew most of the adults in Eagle Valley used to be Protectors, but they weren't in the same shape they were during their twenties.

Then again, maybe Grace was on to something. Maybe striking first was our only chance to end this war. Maybe—with Grace's guidance—we could finally eliminate the demons and bring peace to this realm.

I just couldn't shake the feeling that we were going about it all wrong. Something in my gut told me we were about to make a terrible mistake.

"I'm staying the night at Allie's," I told my mom when I arrived home that night.

I was already up the stairs and halfway to my room when she stopped me.

"Hold on, Kathryn." Mom stopped at the top of the stairs with her hands on her hips. "Do you mind telling me where you've been all day?"

I paused in the hall. I didn't want to look at her. Allie had enough makeup in her locker to help cover up the bruises, but I still feared Mom would notice the swelling.

I sighed and turned to her. "I was at school."

"And after school?" she asked.

I shrugged. "I told you this morning I was doing Davina stuff."

"But you never told me when you'd be home," she pointed out. "You *need* to start answering my text messages."

My thigh heated where my phone sat in my pocket.

Someone had found it at the back doors of the school, where Malcolm had attacked me. Fletcher returned it to me when I'd gone to help in the hospital wing after Grace's announcement, but the screen had been cracked beyond repair.

"Sorry," I said. "I didn't get any of your messages. My phone broke."

Mom frowned. "You need to be more responsible."

My mouth hung open. She wouldn't be saying that if she knew what happened to me earlier.

"Mom, I'm fine," I insisted. "I'll just be next door tonight. It's not a big deal."

Mom crossed her arms. "No, I think you can stay home tonight."

I let out a breath. I wanted to stay at Allie's so we could head straight to the battle together in the morning. I didn't want to be alone the night before we went to war. Of course, I couldn't tell Mom that. She'd mentioned more than once that she didn't want me fighting at all. I'd never make it out of the house if she knew.

"But, Mom—"

"No *buts*. I'm sick of you *telling* me what you're going to do instead of asking my permission. You can stay in your room tonight and think about what it means to respect your mother."

Was she serious?

Mom looked at me with a pointed expression, waiting for my reaction.

"Whatever. I can't wait to get out of here for good." I turned to my bedroom and slammed the door behind me.

In my room, I fell onto my bed. I couldn't believe how controlling my mom could be sometimes. Didn't she realize I was old enough to make my own decisions? I had half a mind to follow her downstairs and tell her just what I thought of her stupid rules.

The sound of voices outside caught my attention. I stood and looked out my window to see Marek and Kyle heading up the walkway to Allie's house.

Great. They were all going to hang out without me, and Mom wanted to keep me trapped in here.

To hell with her.

I grabbed my backpack from the foot of my bed and hurried to my dresser to grab a change of clothes. I slung the bag over my shoulder and opened my window. I was *so* going to get in trouble if Mom found out. But I didn't care. I stepped out of the window onto the shingled porch roof.

"Hey!" Kyle called across the lawn when he saw me.

"Shh…" I hissed as I quietly slid my window shut.

"Whatcha doing up there?" Kyle asked.

"Shut up!" I whisper-yelled. "Unless you want to alert my mom."

I hurried across the roof and lay on my stomach at the edge. My legs found the porch support, and I shimmied my way down it onto the porch railing. I jumped onto the grass and then stole a glance in the front window to see that my mom was occupied in front of the TV. Hopefully, she wouldn't check on me.

I turned away and raced across the lawn to Kyle and Marek. Marek laughed and held his arm out toward me. I wrapped my arm around his waist.

"I'm a bad influence, aren't I?" he teased.

I shrugged. "I think I can figure out how to sneak out on my own."

"But you wouldn't have snuck out if you didn't want to hang out with me," he said lightheartedly.

"Very true," I agreed, smiling up at him.

"Hey!" Allie greeted enthusiastically at the door.

I sniffed the air, and my stomach twisted in hunger. "Is that pizza I smell?"

"Yep," Allie said with a smile. "And ice cream for dessert."

This totally beat another bowl of cereal for dinner with my mom.

Allie put in a dumb slapstick comedy while we ate. Kyle stretched out on the couch, while Allie lay on the floor beneath him. Marek and I sat cuddled on the loveseat together.

Kyle was the last to finish his ice cream. He stood and headed back into the kitchen for another bowl. While he was gone, the rest of us burst into laughter at one of the jokes in the movie.

Kyle raced back into the room at lightning speed, his empty bowl still in his hand. "What'd I miss?"

"You wouldn't have missed it if you weren't such a glutton," Allie teased.

"I'm not a glutton!" Kyle exaggerated his offense. "I *need* to eat a lot. I'm a growing man."

Allie's hand slapped over her mouth as she tried to hide her laugh. "Man? You should be a comedian."

Kyle dropped his bowl on the end table and bent to

swipe the throw pillow out from under Allie's head. A *thud* came as her skull connected with the carpet.

"Ow!" she complained, springing to her feet. "Give it back, Kyle." She reached for the pillow, but Kyle held it high above his head. She punched him so lightly in the ribs that he probably didn't feel a thing. "Jerk."

Marek's shoulders shook next to me in laughter. The movie continued in the background, forgotten.

"Are they always like this?" I whispered.

"Only when they're flirting," he teased.

Allie stood on the sofa and jumped onto Kyle's back. She could've easily reached the pillow, but instead, she used her weight to throw Kyle off balance and tackle him to the couch.

"This is how they flirt?" I asked.

"Yeah," Marek said. "How do you flirt?"

I batted my eyelashes to demonstrate. "Is it working?"

Marek bit his bottom lip, like he was trying to hold back a smile. "Maybe…"

Something in his eyes told me he wanted to kiss me. Nerves fluttered in my gut. *I should just kiss him. He's my boyfriend. I can kiss him whenever I want.*

A high-pitched screech across the room stole my attention. I looked toward Allie and Kyle, thinking Allie accidentally got hurt. Then I realized the noise had come from Kyle.

Growing man my ass. This guy had the falsetto of a ten year old.

Allie sat on top of Kyle and dug her fingers into his ribs. He squealed but made no effort to push her off, even though he was twice as strong. Kyle continued to hold the pillow out of Allie's reach.

"A little help here," Kyle begged between giggles.

I exchanged a smile with Marek and hopped out of the loveseat. I stood at the edge of the couch and ran my fingers across Kyle's bare feet.

"Not like that!" he cried.

While I had Kyle momentarily distracted, Allie lunged forward and snatched the pillow out of his hands. She rolled onto the floor and pulled the pillow to her chest.

Kyle kicked his foot out and narrowly missed my nose.

Without warning, my legs swooped out from under me, and I was suddenly four feet off the ground.

"Whoa there," Marek said into my ear as he cradled me in his arms. "We don't need a broken nose."

"Hey, put me down," I demanded.

Marek only took it as an invitation to toss me over his shoulder.

"*You're* going to end up with a broken nose if you don't put me down." The words escaped between laughs, making me sound anything but serious.

"Am I?" he feigned innocence. The next second, his fingers were tickling the soles of my feet.

"Unfair!" I giggled. My legs flailed, and I beat my hands against his back, but it didn't seem to faze him. "Put me down."

"As you wish." Marek dropped me onto the loveseat, but my hands tangled into the fabric of his t-shirt. He lost his balance and caught himself a split second before he crushed me.

I breathed heavily. His body hovered above mine, his lips only inches away. His t-shirt had ridden up, displaying his hard abs. If Allie and Kyle weren't in the room, I might've ripped the shirt the rest of the way off.

Marek's eyes traveled down to my lips. He was probably thinking the same thing I was.

"This part is hilarious," Allie said, pulling our attention back to the TV.

I reluctantly sat up so Marek could sit beside me. Curling my legs under me, I snuggled into his arms. I inhaled his familiar scent and focused on the soothing rise and fall of his chest. My body completely relaxed into his. I couldn't remember the last time I felt this happy.

As the night wore on, my happiness faded. Soon, images of battle invaded my mind.

I squeezed my eyes shut and forced down the lump in my throat. Marek's delicate feather sat between my fingers, close to my heart. It was in that moment that I realized that one day, this feather might be all I had left of him. This happy night with my friends was only an illusion—a distraction.

Tomorrow, any one of us could die.

I woke in Marek's arms the next morning, feeling more refreshed than I had in a long time. Thank god Allie's dad hadn't kicked the guys out last night. I really needed those hours curled up in Marek's arms.

Marek's head rested against the plush armrest of the loveseat we cuddled on. He stirred and cleared his throat. "Good morning, beautiful."

I smiled and sat up straighter. "You think I'm beautiful?"

He placed a kiss on my nose, sending my heart fluttering. "Of course I do."

I stared into Marek's blue eyes. I could lie here for hours just looking at him.

Something soft bounced off my head. I whirled around so fast that I almost fell off the loveseat. The pillow Kyle had thrown at my head lay on the floor. A light from the kitchen cast shadows over the living room.

"Snap out of it, lovebirds," he said as he bent to tie his shoe. "It's almost time to go."

Tension immediately returned to my shoulders. Right. The fight.

My friends and I were ready to go before sunrise. Allie's dad joined us outside, where the air was cold enough to cause goosebumps to break out over my arms. Marek wore nothing on his upper body but my feather necklace. He must've been freezing. Kyle and Jay were also shirtless.

Wings grew from Jay's back.

"Are we flying?" I asked.

Jay shrugged. "Grace flies everywhere. I don't think she minds."

Everyone else seemed to agree with him and shifted into their Davina form. I felt like they should be a little more wary of exposing themselves, but it was like they didn't think there would be any consequences now that Grace was around. I summoned my wings and followed behind them.

We arrived just as the first rays of sunlight began to light the cloudy sky. There were already at least a hundred Davina in the valley, and more were flooding in. Everyone was dressed to fight. Most guys had their shirts off, and the women wore tank tops so it'd be easy to fly at a moment's notice.

I noticed several guys from school had painted white wings across their bodies. Some had black strips under their eyes like football players. They stood in a circle chanting *Da-vin-a, Da-vin-a.*

I stopped in my tracks. Did they think this was a *game?* This was nothing like the mock battles we had during school. This was real life. People were going to die today.

They might die today. And they were treating it like some sort of sporting event. My gut twisted.

I turned to Marek. He watched the group of chanting guys, almost like he wanted to join them.

"What is it now, Ryn?" Kyle sounded annoyed.

I realized my brows were tight, giving away my uncertainty. I forced myself to relax.

"I—" I didn't know what to say. Yesterday, it seemed like a good idea to strike first. Now, I wasn't so sure. We should be worrying about the people we were going to lose, not cheering for the ones we would kill.

"I'm just wondering if this is the right answer," I said.

"What other answer is there?" Kyle asked. "Think of all the demons you've met. Dorian. Trenton. Malcolm. Each one's just as bad as the next."

I sighed heavily. "Maybe… but—"

"Don't you want this war to end?" Allie sounded genuinely curious.

"Well, yeah," I answered.

"Then let Grace do her job," Kyle said.

"Lay off her, Kyle," Marek defended. "She hasn't been preparing for this as long as you have."

I shot Marek a grateful expression then turned back to Kyle. "I just don't get it. All the stories you told me said Grace would wake when a portal was opening and threatened our realm—and that she'd be able to close it. None of the stories said anything about her rising up against the demons and killing them off."

"They attacked us first," Kyle pointed out.

"I'm sure Grace *is* worrying about the portal," Allie said.

"But these demons are a bigger threat right now. We need to fight them before they attack Eagle Valley again."

If they're such a threat, why'd we waste a whole day "training"?

"I want peace just as much as any Davina," I stated. "I was just saying, maybe there's an alternative. Are you actually *excited* about killing them?"

"Who wouldn't be excited?" A deep voice came from behind me.

I turned to find the group of guys from school making their way over to us. Half of them were in my combat class. The guy who spoke was at least three inches taller than Marek, and his biceps were as big as my head.

Marek's jaw tightened. "No one asked you, Gabe."

I slowly reached out for Marek's fingers.

"Ryn's just scared," Gabe accused without sympathy. "Mr. Collins was right to be skeptical about you."

I narrowed my eyes. "I'm not *scared*. And I think I proved myself a time or two in his class."

"You need to stop having such a big head," Gabe jeered. "So you woke Grace. Big deal."

The guys around him nodded in agreement.

My expression momentarily faltered. "I didn't realize everyone knew it was me."

Gabe crossed his arms. "Secrets don't stay secret for long here in Eagle Valley. You don't realize how many people talk about you, do you?"

I glanced to my friends. Guilt settled on Allie's face, like she knew and just never told me.

"What are you talking about?" I demanded.

Gabe scoffed. "Everyone knows you've conjured essence in front of humans more than once. We know you were kidnapped yesterday."

Freaking small towns.

"So?" I challenged.

Gabe smirked. "So, it's clear you have a thing or two to learn about being a Davina."

Marek stepped forward. "Seriously, Gabe. Back off."

Gabe ignored him. "Face it, Ryn. You're not important anymore."

I gritted my teeth. That's what Gabe thought this was about? That I wanted *attention?*

"That's not what—" I started, but Grace's voice cut me off.

"Davina," she called.

Everyone quieted and turned to her. Her large white wings rose up behind her.

"Thank you for joining us today," Grace said. "I hope that everyone has had a chance to rest, because it's time to give the Aedes what they deserve. They killed your friends and family. And now, we will do the same to them!"

"*Da-vin-a!*" Gabe shouted beside me.

The crowd joined in until the word *Davina* echoed throughout the valley. All around me, wings sprung out of people's backs in preparation for flight.

Marek gazed down at me and squeezed my hand. "Don't worry. This is what Galen High has been preparing us for. We've been training to become Protectors. It's time we finally get our chance to protect."

Marek's words echoed in my mind. At the mention of protection, my thoughts wandered to my mom. If I didn't do this, she—and everyone in Eagle Valley—would be in danger.

"Are you ready?" Marek asked.

Grace spread her wings and shot into the air. All around us, Davina followed.

Nerves fluttered in my gut, but Marek was right. We had to protect Eagle Valley, no matter what it took. I stretched out my wings and joined my fellow Davina in the sky.

Wings flapped all around me. No one seemed to worry about being seen as we flew over the corn fields and tree-tops outside of Eagle Valley. Something about flying with so many other Davina was empowering. Up here, moving as one unit, I had to believe that, together, we were capable of anything.

Up ahead, a patch of forest lay between two corn fields. Just as I spotted it, the Davina at the front of the group dove toward the trees. The rest of our group followed in a spiral, as if warning the demons of the impending danger we sought to bring down upon them.

Screams filled the air when the Davina landed and immediately jumped into combat. Some were shrieks of warning, others of pain. Most sounded like the cries of eager Davina pumped for battle. Demons scattered.

Marek stayed close to me, and together, we raced through the thin forest, knocking out demon after demon. Several Protectors followed behind us and quickly finished off the demons we'd stunned. Some turned to snapping necks. Others used the Davina Blades they'd brought with them.

Ahead of us, I spotted Fletcher engaged in combat with a tall demon. Beyond him, a flash of purple caught my eye. I paused, momentarily distracted by Grace's essence. It was nothing like the essence I'd used when I had access to her power. Purple lightning blasted out of her hands like a stream of water shooting out of a firehose. She shocked four demons at once. Before I could process what just happened, they were gone.

"Ryn, come on!" Marek grabbed my hand.

I sprinted behind him, deeper into the middle of the fight. Without warning, a demon jumped out from behind a tree straight in front of me. I rammed into him and fell to the ground.

Marek didn't miss a beat. He knocked the demon to the forest floor and slammed his head against the ground. I quickly got to my feet and readied myself for whatever came next.

"Behind you!" Marek called.

I whirled around and sank my foot into a demon's stomach. He stumbled back a few feet and fell to the ground. His hood dropped.

All around me, the sound of battle faded, and it felt as if *I'd* been kicked in the gut. I stared, shocked and horrified, into the demon's face. It wasn't a man at all.

A young girl looked up at me, her dark eyes filled with fear. She couldn't be more than twelve years old. An image of Emily's face flashed across my vision as I stared down at the girl. Emily, the fifteen-year-old training partner we'd lost in the last battle. It suddenly occurred to me that the demons weren't all like Clinton, Dorian, and Malcolm. Some of them were like Emily—young, scared, and innocent.

The girl hesitated for a moment. I could see it in her eyes. She thought this was the end for her, that I was going to beat the living shit out of her until her final breath.

And I knew I wouldn't touch her.

When she saw I wasn't about to pounce on her and snap her neck, she scurried to her feet and raced away. But she only made it a few yards before a strong male Davina gripping a blade crossed in front of her and slit her throat.

"No!" My knees grew weak.

The Davina continued fighting like it didn't even faze him.

I rushed over to the girl and caught her as she collapsed. She wheezed, struggling to suck air into her lungs. I pressed my hands to her throat to try to stop the bleeding, but it was too late. Dark blood spurted from her throat and coated my hands.

"No, no, no," I mumbled under my breath. "I'm so sorry. This isn't fair to you."

The girl looked up at me but gave no indication that she heard my apology. Her eyes glistened with tears and the pain of war. In her terrified expression, I could read what she'd say to me if she could.

Why?

And then she went limp. Her weight in my arms vanished the moment her body disappeared in a puff of black smoke. Her cloak draped over my arms. It remained the only reminder that she had, in fact, been real.

I sat there for far too long, staring down at the empty cloak in my hands. If any demon had noticed me amidst the chaos, they could have easily snuck up behind me and killed me on the spot. But no one seemed to care about the Davina girl mourning for one of her enemies.

My hands shook as I used the girl's cloak to wipe my skin clean of her blood. The forest slowly came into focus again. By now, the screams and chaos had died down. I glanced around me to see that only Davina remained. The demons had either run off to save themselves or had died trying.

Marek rushed over to me and dropped to his knees. "Ryn, are you okay?"

I swallowed hard. "It's over already?"

It almost seemed unfair how much devastation we could deliver in such a short amount of time. Black cloaks lay scattered across the forest floor, and Davina trampled over them like they were of no consequence.

And then I spotted the bodies. The Davina bodies, the people the demons managed to kill before they scattered. I rose to my feet and started toward the closest body. It was a small figure with dark black hair.

Please don't let it be someone I know. Don't be Allie.

Relief and pain washed over me all at once. It wasn't Allie, but I was all too familiar with the young boy's face.

Ethan.

My chest felt empty. Another member of our training team… gone.

"I told him he was too young for this." My voice cracked.

Marek stared down at Ethan and spoke quietly. "I know. But this is war, Ryn."

I had a feeling he was saying that to reassure himself. It was like convincing himself it was all worth it to eliminate the Aedes was the only way he'd be able to stomach it.

I buried my face in Marek's chest. "I don't want to lose anyone I love."

"I don't, either," Marek whispered. His strong hands ran up and down my back. "Let's go find Allie and Kyle, to make sure they're all right."

I opened my mouth to agree, but before I got a word out, cheers erupted toward the other end of the forest. I turned to see a large group surrounding Grace, celebrating our victory.

As Marek and I stepped closer to the crowd, Grace struggled to push her way out of the group. Finally, she broke free, but celebration around her continued. Grace stumbled forward and caught herself against the trunk of a nearby tree. Color had drained from her face, and she looked as if she might vomit. Grace kept her eyes on the ground without regarding the dead bodies she passed.

An invisible force tugged at my heart. I felt for her. She acted like she didn't think we should be celebrating when we had yet to mourn for our fallen Davina. I felt the same way.

I rushed toward Grace to offer my sympathies. Marek followed behind me but didn't say anything.

"Grace," I called when I was several paces away from her.

She lifted her head, and her eyes met mine. Her expression remained neutral, like she was trying to hide her true feelings.

"Grace, are you okay?" I asked.

What am I saying? Of course she's not okay. She just led a handful of her own people to their deaths. That's not something you come out of feeling *okay* about.

Grace straightened and held her head high. She took a breath to say something but sighed instead, as if contemplating how to express her feelings. "This will all be over soon, Ryn. Then, we will finally be at peace."

Grace turned away from me without another word. I stared after her speechlessly. The way she said it, it almost sounded like she was already at peace. Something told me she'd accepted that her death would come sooner than later.

A scary thought hit me. Maybe this battle wasn't the first step in winning this war after all. Maybe it was a test for Grace.

And maybe she found her answer.

ollowing the battle, Davina slowly began to return to Eagle Valley. Several stayed to assist the injured, and a group of Davina came back with vans to help transport the fallen home. Allie, Kyle, and Marek lifted dead bodies into one of the vans. I couldn't take looking at their lifeless faces.

Instead, I walked through the forest, gathering the cloaks that lay forgotten. The metallic scent of blood filled my nose. Allie shot me a somber expression, but other Davina eyed me skeptically, wondering why I bothered. I wasn't sure I had an answer. It just didn't seem right to leave them, like the Aedes we killed didn't matter. I tried not to count the cloaks draped over my forearm.

I dropped the pile of cloaks at the edge of the trees and then headed back into the forest to gather more. Once I collected all the cloaks I could find, I laid each one in a line beside each other. I didn't know if the Aedes would return here or not, but if they did, at least they wouldn't have to do this themselves. I hoped it would be easier for them to mourn their lost this way.

By the time I finished, the vans had pulled away from the shoulder of the road, and only my friends and I remained at the scene of the battle.

"How many did we lose?" I asked as I slumped over to my friends.

Allie dropped her head. "Too many."

I was glad she didn't give me an exact answer.

"Should we head back?" Marek suggested.

I nodded solemnly and flexed my shoulders to summon my wings. The flight back to Eagle Valley took a good ten minutes at top speed. We landed in the valley and walked the rest of the way back to the school. Davina swarmed the lawn behind the mansion, dancing, singing, and celebrating our hard-won victory.

I didn't know how they did it. No one acted like this after our last battle. It was like they were already becoming immune to it, like they were losing a piece of their humanity.

Kyle joined the group celebrating, and Allie followed behind him. Marek hesitated beside me.

"Go ahead," I told him. "I need to find Fletcher and talk to him."

"I don't want to leave you alone," Marek said.

"I'll be fine," I assured him. "There are enough Davina here."

"There were plenty of Davina around last time, too," Marek pointed out. "At least let me stay with you until you find him."

"Okay," I agreed.

Marek and I walked through the crowd for fifteen minutes without spotting Fletcher. When we couldn't find him outside, we entered the mansion. Marek stopped at his locker to grab an extra t-shirt before we headed upstairs to check the hospital wing.

Several more cots had been added to provide rest for the newly injured Davina. My heart sank when I saw volunteers rushing around the room, trying to treat the injured as fast as they could. While everyone else was outside celebrating, our injured were in here suffering, and the volunteers were swamped.

I spotted Fletcher across the room, holding onto a woman's hand as two others tried to stitch up a large gash across her swollen face.

I didn't want to bother Fletcher while he was busy. Instead, Marek and I helped where we could. We filled patients' water bottles and adjusted pillows. I helped a girl with a cast on her leg to the bathroom.

It was several hours before things calmed down enough that I felt confident bothering Fletcher. Nerves twisted in my gut when I approached him.

"Hey, Fletcher," I said. "Can we talk?"

Fletcher looked exhausted, but he nodded anyway. "I heard they put out a salad bar a few hours ago in the cafeteria. Should we go get something to eat?"

Marek was too noble to stop volunteering, so he stayed in the hospital wing while Fletcher and I headed downstairs. The cafeteria was empty, but there was still food out at the salad bar. I filled up my tray—even though the lettuce had wilted slightly. Fletcher and I sat across from each other at the table farthest from the doors.

Fletcher stabbed into his salad. "What is it you want to talk about, Ryn?"

I poked at my food, but I couldn't bring myself to eat it. "Here's the thing…"

I couldn't find the words.

"Yes?" Fletcher prodded.

I took a deep breath. "I feel awful about what we did. There were *kids* fighting in that battle. We killed children. I watched an Aedes girl die, Fletcher. She looked *terrified*. I'm not sure if she was that much different from the innocent Davina we lost today."

"The Aedes *are* different, Ryn," Fletcher stated.

"But maybe they're not as bad as everyone thinks they are," I argued. "Maybe we can…"

I trailed off. I suspected Fletcher would only laugh at me if I suggested we could make peace with the Aedes.

Fletcher rested his fork on his tray. "Ryn, I realize that you don't have a lot of experience with the Aedes and that you view them through a different lens than the rest of us do. But, perhaps the lens in which you view them is misguided."

My brows came together. "You think it's misguided for me to believe there has to be an alternative to all this?"

Fletcher sighed heavily. "The Aedes can't be reasoned with."

"No one's tried—"

"Let me tell you a story," Fletcher cut in. He rested his elbows on the table and brought his fingers together in front of his face. "Like most Davina, I was a Protector in my early twenties. I was very good at what I did. I killed a lot of Aedes, but it only takes one moment, one mistake, to change everything."

I fell silent and listened to what he had to say.

"I was married then. We were both Protectors and fought alongside each other. I was a Protector, but I wasn't able to protect *her*—or our son."

Fletcher's confession was like a slap in the face. I had no idea something so terrible happened to him.

"I thought you said you didn't have any kids," I pointed out.

Fletcher shook his head. "Not anymore. My family died at the hands of an Aedes."

My heart sank. After all this time, it was clear the topic still caused him pain to speak about.

Fletcher paused for a beat before continuing. "I wanted revenge, to hunt down the Aedes that killed her, but instead, I gave up being a Protector. I came back to Eagle Valley and started teaching. I thought that by doing so, I could help future generations from making similar mistakes."

"What was her mistake?" I asked curiously.

Fletcher's gaze dropped. "It wasn't her mistake. It was mine."

An inaudible gasp passed my lips.

"I let an Aedes go," Fletcher admitted. "He was the first one to beg me to spare him, and I fell for it. He repaid me by killing my family."

We both fell quiet. The only sound I heard was the hum of the freezers in the adjoining kitchen.

"Fletcher," I whispered. "I'm so sorry."

He straightened up. "It was a long time ago."

"That doesn't make it any less significant," I told him.

Fletcher didn't meet my gaze. "No, I suppose it doesn't. I just hope that you, Ryn, will not keep yourself from recognizing the threats out there."

I wasn't sure how to respond.

"Most of us have lost people we love to the Aedes," Fletcher said. "Perhaps now, with Grace back, we can finally end it."

"Maybe," I said flatly, "but how many people are we going to have to sacrifice in the process? We're losing people we love as we speak."

Fletcher's lips tightened. "And we'd lose more if we left this alone."

"I wasn't suggesting—"

"The Aedes are evil," Fletcher declared. "We finally have a chance at exterminating them."

Fletcher didn't seem to be listening. That, or he didn't care. Grace was supposed to return when the line between the realms was thinning. If that was the case now, it wouldn't matter how many Aedes we killed first. They'd quickly outnumber us.

It sure felt like I wasn't the only one who was misguided around here.

~

I found Allie sitting on the back steps of the mansion, staring out into the distance. It'd been a long day, and the sun hung low in the sky. The group from earlier had thinned, but others stuck around, still looking positively pleased with the victory. I sat beside Allie, but she kept her eyes on the lawn, never looking at me.

"Hey, Allie. How's it been going out here?"

She shrugged and looked down at her feet.

"What's going on?" I asked.

Allie shrugged again.

"I can tell you're not okay. Please don't shut me out." I scooted closer to her and wrapped my arm around her shoulder. "With everything that's happening, we need each other now more than ever."

Allie shook her head, like she didn't want to tell me. "It's nothing. I'm just… not feeling very much like celebrating."

Did I detect a hint of regret in Allie's tone?

I spotted Kyle with a group of guys shooting essence at each other and dodging it like it was a game. They didn't even seem to care they were out here in the open, like they knew the end of the world was coming and so the secret of our magic didn't matter anymore.

I wondered if that's why they acted so cheerful—because they weren't certain if they'd be the ones to die in the next battle and they were trying to have as much fun as they could.

When I finally spoke again, my voice came out small. "Do you think we did the right thing?"

"What do you mean?" Allie asked.

"Attacking the Aedes," I clarified.

"Of course," she answered. It sounded like an automatic response. "If we didn't kill them first, they'd kill us. That's how they work." She swallowed. "That's what happened to my mom."

I didn't say anything further. Allie was hurting right now, and I knew she wouldn't listen to what I had to say.

I sensed Marek's approach before he sat beside me on the concrete steps.

"Hey," he said lightly. "How are you two?"

Allie glanced at him and shrugged.

"I think everyone's just really tired," I said. I knew I was.

Marek kept his eyes on Allie's fallen face. "You okay?"

"Yeah," she replied, but it didn't sound genuine. "Like you said, I'm just tired. I think I'm going to go get Kyle and head home." Allie rose to her feet.

I stood beside her. "I'm ready to go, too."

"I'll take you home," Marek offered. The way he looked at me told me he wanted us to talk alone.

"Okay," I agreed. I turned back to Allie and pulled her into a hug. "I'll see you later. Make sure to get lots of sleep."

"Thanks. I'll try." She offered a half-hearted smile then headed across the lawn toward Kyle.

I turned back to Marek just as he pulled his t-shirt over his head. His wings grew behind him.

"We're flying?" I asked.

He nodded, and a slight smile touched his lips. "Come on."

Marek pumped his wings and launched himself into the air. I hesitated only a moment before following.

11

We landed outside of town on a rocky hilltop, the hill where Marek and I shared our first kiss. The sun touched the horizon, and most of the cloud cover had disappeared. A light breeze rustled through the trees surrounding the small clearing.

Marek pulled his wings into him and put his t-shirt back on. He sat on the large slab of granite and reached an arm out to me, inviting me to join him. The tension in my shoulders eased when I snuggled into his warm chest. The nighttime was peaceful in contrast to the bloody day that came before.

Eventually, Marek broke the silence. "What's wrong, Ryn?"

My mouth grew dry. "Nothing," I lied.

How could he tell?

"You know that's not true. Today was hard on you." There was no question in his voice. "Do you want to talk about it?"

I dropped my gaze to my feet. "Not really."

He'll just brush me off like Fletcher did.

Marek tightened his arm around me. "You can tell me anything."

I wanted to believe that so badly. I pulled away from him, and his arm dropped from around my shoulder.

I knotted my hands together. "I know that, but I can't always predict how you'll react."

"Please talk to me," he pleaded.

I couldn't refuse the look in his eyes, but my heart began to hammer as I prepared for the confession. "Okay… The thing is, I feel uneasy. Everyone's acting like the battle meant nothing, and they're using Grace to justify killing. But Marek, I'm not sure we should trust her."

His brow furrowed. "Why wouldn't you trust her?"

I sighed. "See, this is why I didn't want to say anything. You're acting the same as everyone else. And now you think I'm being stupid."

"I don't think that at all." He placed his arm around my shoulder again, but I didn't lean into him.

"I don't get why we have to *kill* them," I said. "Can't we compromise?"

Marek's lips turned down. "I think it's a little unrealistic."

"Is it, though?" I asked. "Has anyone ever tried? You said they're not a community race, but now they've finally come together. Maybe if we could talk to their leader, the rest of them will listen."

Marek stared out across Eagle Valley. "Maybe Grace could—"

"No," I said too quickly.

Marek shot me a questioning glance.

"I'm not sure Grace *wants* peace," I explained. "It feels like… like she's up to something."

Marek eyed me skeptically.

I pressed my lips together. "Isn't it a little strange that she hasn't mentioned the portal at all? I thought she came back because the Aedes's realm was about to open. It's like she's distracting us with training and ideas of war when none of it matters. So maybe she doesn't know where the portal is. Or maybe she *wants* Aedes to flood our realm."

"Or she's just trying to help us eliminate the most immediate threat—the demons that attacked Eagle Valley," Marek suggested. "Or maybe she never came back because a portal was opening. She said she's been observing all this time. Maybe she came back to help us win this war."

"Then why not return sooner?" I argued.

Marek thought about it for a moment. "Maybe she knows things she doesn't want to talk about publicly."

I sighed. "This is why I didn't want to talk about it. You won't listen to me."

"I *am* listening," Marek assured me. "I'm just trying to understand better."

My jaw tightened. "I don't know what else to say, Marek. I just don't get why everyone's mindlessly following Grace. I watched an Aedes girl die in my arms today. I can't believe everyone is okay with murdering children."

Marek sat still for several minutes, considering my

words. We were both silent for so long that I thought maybe that was the end of the conversation.

Finally, he spoke. "I think you might have a point."

Excitement rushed through me. Finally, someone actually listened!

"About which part?" I asked.

"That we should try negotiating peace first," Marek answered. "I just don't know how we'd do it and how we'd get Grace to listen to us. And I'm not sure it would solve all our problems anyway. After all, the demons aren't the only ones who are evil."

A sense of *deja vu* hit.

"You've said that before," I said gently. "What do you mean by it?"

Marek's features hardened, like he suddenly realized he'd said too much. "I just mean… anyone can be evil."

My heart dropped. Was Marek *ever* going to open up to me? I'd told him all of my secrets. But I knew better than to push it or guilt him into telling me, so I didn't say anything.

"Let's forget about it for tonight. Right now, it's just you…" Marek placed a light kiss on the top of my head. "… and me… alone."

I titled my head up to look into his eyes. His warm breath rushed across my cheek, awakening the butterflies in my stomach. What was he suggesting?

His lips brushed across my forehead. "I hate seeing you like this. I wish I could make it better."

My face heated, and I shied away. He was trying to distract me. And dammit, it was working.

He bent and touched his lips to the side of my mouth.

Worries fell from my mind as I surrendered to his touch. I didn't have a chance to breathe between each kiss he placed on my lips. My hands tangled in his hair, and I pulled him closer to me.

I wanted more. I wanted all of him.

I never took my lips off his as I got to my knees and climbed into his lap. His strong hands settled on my hips. I reached for the hem of his shirt and pushed the fabric out of the way so my hands could run along the hard muscles in his abdomen. I'd seen him shirtless plenty of times, but it was different to touch him, to feel him.

Marek's shirt rode up above his pecks as I ran my hands up his chest and then across his back. He pulled away momentarily and lifted his arms, inviting me to strip the shirt off from him.

I gladly complied. I tossed his shirt beside us and began trailing kisses down his neck. My lips touched the necklace I'd given him.

Marek wrapped a strong arm around my middle. He whirled me onto the ground and kissed me like he couldn't control himself. His hands rode up my tank top, and I wrapped my legs around his hips.

You can touch me if you want, I wanted to say to him, but I was afraid I'd ruin the moment if I spoke. Instead, I let him explore my body at his own pace.

Marek's fingers grazed across the underwire of my bra.

Take it off already, I begged silently.

My heart hammered violently against the inside of my rib cage, like it was trying to pound its way out of my chest and into Marek's hands. I squeezed my legs tighter around his hips to let him know he had my permission to take things as far as he wanted.

A moment later, he pulled away.

"What's wrong?" I asked in a rushed, breathy voice.

Marek reached for his shirt and balled it into his hand. "It's getting late. We should get you home."

"My curfew isn't for another few hours." I reached out for him, but he pushed my hands away.

What the hell?

After everything we'd been through and all the sacrifices I made for him, he was still holding back from loving me? I'd *killed* for him! Didn't that count for something?

I pushed myself to my elbows and spoke softly. "Did I do something wrong?"

He shook his head, but it was hard to see his expression through the darkness.

"Then why'd you stop?" I asked.

Marek reached out a hand and helped me to my feet. "It's just..."

Cool air brushed across my exposed midsection. I tugged down on my tank top to settle the fabric back into place.

What part of this wasn't perfect for him?

"Marek?" I reached out to lace my fingers through his.

He turned away and summoned his wings, like he hadn't noticed. "Let's get you home."

That's how this is going to go?

My lips tightened, but I followed his instructions. It was clear I wasn't going to get a real answer from him.

We landed in the shadows on my back lawn several minutes later, but it felt like hours of silence had passed between us.

"Marek," I started, but my throat closed up around my words.

Marek stepped forward and took my hand. "Get some rest. I'll see you tomorrow."

He bent and placed a chaste kiss on my cheek. I was sure it was meant to make me feel better, but after the moment we shared at the top of our hill, it felt like an insult.

Marek turned and launched himself into the air, leaving me standing alone in my back yard. My chest tightened with each passing moment that I stared after him. I didn't know why Marek was shutting me out.

In that moment, I realized that I had no idea what my future with Marek held. All I wanted was for him to open up to me, but I knew with certainty that if he couldn't be honest with me, our relationship was doomed for failure.

I'd never be ready for the moment we eventually crashed and burned.

12

After Marek's disappointing departure that night and another pointless argument with my mom, I'd just about had it with everyone's shit.

It didn't matter that I was still exhausted from the sleepless night I had. I rose early and dragged my tired ass to Galen High, intent on finding Grace. One way or another, I'd get her to listen to me.

The school was unusually quiet for a Wednesday morning. After yesterday's battle, we were supposed to start a more rigorous training program, but so far, a new schedule hadn't been issued. In my book, that meant school had been effectively canceled until Grace and the Davina Council figured things out.

When I didn't find Grace in the hospital wing, I tried the valley. Three small groups of Davina practiced their skills below me, but I didn't see Grace anywhere.

I turned to head back to the school but rammed straight into someone. I stepped back a few paces and looked up to

88

see Gabe staring down at me. Several Davina from school stopped behind him. My eyes caught Casey's for a brief moment. Apparently, she'd found a new group of Davina to hang out with.

I tried to step around Gabe, but he moved to the side to block my path.

"Where ya going?" Gabe taunted. "You're not headed to cry over another demon, are you?"

Several people laughed behind him. I didn't look to see if Casey was one of them. I wouldn't put it past her, though.

I gritted my teeth. I was *so* not in the mood. "Let me through."

"Why don't you come practice with us?" Gabe's tone was anything but inviting. "It'll help toughen you up. Davina don't cry over demons."

I swallowed hard. "Maybe there's something wrong with that."

I spread my wings and shot myself above the tree line. *To hell with Gabe. And the rest of them.*

"They're only demons," Gabe called after me.

I hardly heard him as I flew over the trees between the school and the valley. I pumped my wings harder and soared above the top of the three-story mansion. I planned to circle around and land near the back doors, but something caught my eye. A dark-skinned woman in a white gown sat in a chair on one of the school's balconies.

I glided down to her. I came in faster than I intended and slammed into the railing. My abdomen caught the bulk of the blow, and I thought for a moment I might puke.

Grace slowly lifted her gaze. Apparently, my horrible landing wasn't as bad as I thought, because she hardly noticed my arrival. I gripped onto the top of the railing and swung my legs over it until I stood on solid ground.

"Hi, Grace," I said like we were old friends.

Her eyes met mine, but it felt as if she was looking through me. Her gaze returned to look out across the empty lawn.

"What can I help you with, Ryn?" she asked softly.

Good to know I'm not invisible.

I leaned against the railing and crossed my arms. I hadn't exactly planned what I was going to say to her. I just knew I had to reason with her *somehow*. If she wasn't going to listen to me, the Aedes sure as hell wouldn't.

I forced my voice out past the lump in my throat. "There's something I want to talk to you about."

Grace didn't respond.

I cleared my throat and continued. "I think we should arrange a meeting with the Aedes to try to come to a peaceful solution."

Grace still didn't say anything. I expected her to object, but it was like she hadn't heard me.

"You were around when the Davina tried to make peace with the Aedes before," I continued. "Maybe we can learn something from your experience and try again. These are different Aedes. Perhaps this time, they'll listen."

I waited several moments for Grace's reply, but she was completely checked out. Just as I was about to snap my fingers in front of her face, she spoke.

"Do you feel that, Ryn?" She closed her eyes and inhaled a deep breath.

I narrowed my eyes. "Feel what?"

"Just hold still and concentrate," she instructed.

I chewed the dry skin on my lower lip but eventually caved. I closed my eyes and listened to my body. All I felt was far too much tension in my shoulders.

I peeled my eyes back open. "I don't feel anything."

"I feel everything," she said without opening her eyes. "I feel the heat of the sun on my skin. I feel the light morning breeze passing though my hair. I hear the birds chirping in the trees and the sound of wind chimes down the street. The heartbeat of every patient in the hospital wing pulses across my skin."

I furrowed my brow. That last part couldn't be true, could it?

Had she heard me at all? What did any of this have to do with the war we were facing?

"What's your point?" I struggled to keep the irritation out of my tone.

Grace finally opened her eyes. "My point is, if you look for it, you'll find peace. Peace is out there, in nature."

"Okay… but that's not going to help us with the Aedes."

Grace tilted her chin toward the rising sun. "No. I never said it would."

This woman was impossible. When did she start speaking in riddles?

I turned to the glass doors beside us. Clearly, she wasn't going to listen to me. Would anyone?

After I abandoned Grace, I found Allie and Kyle in the

hospital wing. I was relieved to see several cots were empty and the rest of the injured Davina seemed to be doing better. Our healing abilities weren't anything short of a miracle.

"Can I get you anything else?" Allie asked as she handed a water bottle to the lady with stitches on her face.

"No, thank you," she answered. "You've helped immensely already."

Allie noticed me for the first time.

"Can we walk?" I suggested.

Allie nodded and left the hospital wing with me. I eyed her as we headed down the stairs. Bags had settled under her eyes, and she hadn't even bothered with makeup today. Allie used to be so excited to become a Protector. Now that day was here, and I wasn't entirely convinced she was cut out for it.

"How are you doing?" I asked her.

"I'm fine." She couldn't hide the lie in her tone. "What about you?"

We reached the bottom of the stairs. Several Davina sat around the fireplace in the common room.

I didn't speak until we passed them and entered the hall behind the grand staircase. "I tried talking to Grace about meeting with the Aedes, but I'm not sure she heard a word I said."

Allie gazed down at her feet while we walked. "I'm sure Grace has a reason for whatever it is she's doing."

It didn't sound like Allie truly believed what she was saying. It was like she said it only to reassure herself because she was so desperate to believe in Grace the way the rest of the Davina did.

"Sure, she has a reason," I said. "But her reason may not be as noble as everyone thinks."

Allie bit the inside of her lip. "Maybe not…"

"Ryn," a familiar voice called.

I stopped in the hall and retreated a few steps before glancing into Fletcher's classroom. My eyes first fell upon Marek standing near Fletcher's desk, but it was Fletcher who had called my name.

I purposely avoided Marek's eyes and looked to Fletcher instead. "Yeah?"

"Come in." Fletcher gestured to Allie and me.

I glanced warily between Marek and Fletcher. Marek's expression remained calm. Was he even bothered by what happened between us last night?

"The Davina Council is looking for people to fly the outskirts of town to watch for any threats from the Aedes," Fletcher said. "I thought maybe you'd be interested in helping out."

I exchanged a glance with Allie. Her face lit up, like she couldn't be happier to get out of here.

"I thought we weren't supposed to fly where humans could see us," I pointed out.

Fletcher frowned. "We shouldn't be, but the Davina Council doesn't seem to care now that Grace is back. She's the one who said she wanted Davina flying out there to guard from another Aedes attack. I'm asking you three— and Kyle, if he wants—to volunteer, because I know you four are competent enough to keep an eye out without making a scene."

Marek nodded. "We'll do our best."

I didn't like how Marek answered like he spoke for the entire group, but I knew I'd follow him anyway. Flying totally beat sitting around Galen doing nothing all day.

Several hours passed as we circled the outskirts of Eagle Valley without spotting a single threat. We flew high above the cornfields near the clouds, where the air was thin and cool.

"How much longer should we patrol?" I shouted toward Marek, who flew several yards away from me.

I couldn't help it when my eyes traveled over his exposed torso. I wanted so badly for him to hold me against his chest, but I didn't know at this point if he *wanted* to hold me. He hadn't given me a clue how he felt all day.

Marek shrugged. "Fletcher never said, but if you're getting tired—"

"Don't be a wimp!" Kyle called out from in front of us. He flipped in the air and quickly caught himself. "I thought you liked flying."

"I do like flying." I quickened my pace to catch up with him.

Kyle raised his eyebrows and sped up to distance himself from me. A challenging look crossed Allie's face as she pushed ahead of him.

"Hey, guys—" Marek started.

His voice was drowned out by the sound of wind rushing past my ears. I pumped my wings harder and passed by Kyle.

"Guys!" Marek called again.

Allie and I exchanged a mischievous glance and sprinted beside each other, swaying one way and then the other to block Kyle from passing us.

"Not fair!" he called.

We dropped lower when he tried to fly beneath us. We weren't racing as much as trying to keep Kyle from getting in the lead. We had no destination and weren't paying attention to where we were going. I was sure Marek yelled at us at least five more times, but it was hard to hear him. The farther we went, the more tuckered out I got. Allie noticed me slowing down.

"Do you need a break?" she called.

I nodded.

Allie turned back to Kyle and Marek and gestured toward the ground. She quickly changed direction and dropped out of the sky. I dove after her. We landed in a large grassy clearing with trees on all sides, and I fell onto my back with my wings spread wide beneath me. Laughter filled my chest.

Marek fell into the grass near my head and reached out to touch my fingers. My initial reaction was to pull away, but I didn't. My eyes met his, and he stared back with an apologetic expression.

"I'm sorry," he whispered. "About last night."

A smile touched my lips. It was a relief to know he wasn't mad at me.

"I'm sorry, too," I replied. "I don't want to fight."

Marek ran his thumb across the back of my hand. "Me, either."

"That was fun!" Allie exclaimed breathlessly, breaking the spell between Marek and me. She hadn't noticed our exchange.

Kyle sat with an elbow rested on his knee. "Ready for another go?"

I lifted my head to look at him. "Give us a second to cool down, would—?"

My voice stopped dead when my eye caught something across the clearing. The air rippled, interrupting the stillness in the clearing and distorting the landscape beyond it. The tree trunks themselves seemed to sway in slight motion. Something was amiss, as if the threads in the fabric of reality as we knew it were unraveling.

"What?" Allie looked at me, then glanced to where my eyes were locked.

Was I imagining it?

Everyone stopped to follow my gaze. If they said anything else, I didn't hear them. I rose to my feet and inched closer to the disturbance. A strange energy grew inside of me the closer I got to it.

"Whoa," Allie said in awe beside me. I hadn't realized everyone else had gotten to their feet and followed.

We stopped mere inches from the ripple. It was hardly visible, but I noticed a swirling of colors in the air the longer I stared. It was the size of a doorway, rising only a foot or two above my head.

Kyle wet his lips and reached out to touch the visible air.

Marek grabbed his wrist before he could make contact. "Don't touch it."

Kyle listened, but I didn't. I felt nothing but air when my fingers connected with the strange phenomenon. The only reason I knew I'd touched it was because of the small ripple that spread out from my fingertips. The air waved in front of us like the surface of a pond.

"You don't think...?" Allie started.

She didn't need to finish her question. I was sure we were all thinking the same thing.

"That it's a portal to the Aedes realm?" I whispered. "*The* portal. The one Grace came back to protect us from? Yeah, I think it is."

Kyle turned to me. "But if a portal has opened, then—"

"I don't know if it's fully open yet," I said.

"How can we know for sure?" Allie asked.

"We could try to step through it," Kyle joked.

"We're not doing that," Marek replied seriously. "We don't have any idea what it could do to us."

"Or what could be waiting for us on the other side," Allie pointed out.

I walked the length of the ripple to view it from every angle.

"This is really strange," Kyle stated.

Allie swatted at him. "Obviously."

"No, I mean, it's strange that there's a portal so close to Eagle Valley," Kyle said.

"It *is* a strange coincidence," Marek agreed.

Or not a coincidence at all, I thought.

"Maybe we're wrong," Allie suggested. "Maybe it's just some strange natural phenomenon."

I stopped pacing. "It's not. This is where the realms touch, and that line is thinning."

Excitement surged through my body. Finally, we were getting somewhere. We could take action.

"We need to get Grace out here before this thing breaks open," I said.

Marek spread his wings wide. "Let's go tell her."

"There's no need for that," a voice said from behind us.

We all whirled around in unison to find Grace standing mere yards from us. What were the chances? There was no time to waste.

"Grace!" I exclaimed. "This is where the realms touch, isn't it?"

Grace nodded.

"You can secure it, can't you?" I asked desperately. "That's why you had me wake you. We can destroy this portal now, before it has a chance to open."

Grace frowned. "I'm afraid I can't do that."

What?

She was the one leading this war against the Aedes. Did she *want* the rest of them to flood this realm and destroy us? A terrifying thought occurred.

"You're on their side!" I accused. "You don't care how many Aedes we kill, as long as you can distract the Davina long enough for a portal to open. Then you'll have enough Aedes to take over this realm! Why would you do that?"

Grace remained calm. "You're terribly mistaken, Ryn."

"Then why won't you destroy this thing?" I yelled.

Grace looked down at her bare feet and stepped toward us. "Ryn, I think it's time that you finally knew the truth."

13

Grace promised we were in for a long story and invited us to sit in the grass while she explained. My friends and I exchanged wary glances before joining Grace on the ground.

I didn't like this. I should be standing, with my wings spread out, so I could take flight at a moment's notice. But I feared Grace wouldn't talk until I did as she instructed.

Grace took a deep breath. "The truth is, the stories you've heard are wrong."

I eyed Grace skeptically. Allie gasped beside me, and Marek and Kyle exchanged a questioning glance.

"The Davina today fear a portal to the Aedes realm because they fear what is on the other side. The Originals feared the portals themselves," Grace explained. "We believe the realms were always unstable but that they became more of a threat after The Great War that killed the gods."

She dropped her gaze. "The gateways between the earth

and Vehena were the first to go. Davina began pouring back into our home realm when we realized the portals were collapsing. The sixteen of us didn't choose to stay behind as your stories say. We were just the last to make it."

I could hear the heartbreak in her tone.

Grace continued. "By the time we reached the last remaining portal, we saw that our realm had turned into a wasteland on the brink of falling completely apart. Our world was dying. The other Davina were already gone. To protect our demolishing realm from affecting the others, the sixteen of us sent our essence into the portal and collapsed it, sealing off the realm. To keep the remaining two realms from destroying each other, we pushed the Aedes back for their own protection and sealed the portals."

"How?" Marek asked curiously. "How did you seal them?"

"Think of the portals like an archway," Grace said. "If you apply enough pressure—essence, in this case—they will collapse."

"How is there one here, though?" Kyle asked. I could tell he was burning for the answer. "How is it this close to Eagle Valley?"

"Long ago, Praesid had records of where the old portals were located," Grace told us. "They used these locations to predict where the new portals might open. Praesid spread the Originals across the globe to the most likely locations. Over time, several portals opened. They were able to plug those locations into the equation and better pinpoint where the next would occur."

"Wait," Marek stopped her. I could tell by the look on his face that we were thinking the exact same thing.

"You mean… the portals have opened before?" I asked in disbelief.

"Yes," Grace answered. "It has happened many times throughout history. On several occasions, other Originals were awakened to protect this realm, but that was before the rest of them died. This is my first time being awakened. It appears that Praesid and the Haylo brothers calculated the next portal properly."

Silence hung in the air as we all considered her story. Marek's uncertain gaze caught mine. Could all of this be true?

"What happened after you sealed the first portals?" Allie asked.

"We knew we wouldn't be safe forever," Grace replied. "The realms had previously been sealed off and reopened when the gods were still alive. The realms touch, and they can create cracks between them. We had an idea of where they might strike next, but we couldn't be sure. To monitor the earth for these events, we sent our consciousness and essence into the earth, freezing our immortal bodies."

I couldn't miss the disbelief that fell over my friends' faces. Her story made so much sense, but it also meant that all the stories they'd grown up believing in were laced in falsehoods. The Davina had lost so much of the truth throughout time.

"Now what do we do?" I asked Grace.

"When this portal opens fully, the realms will collide. It

will destroy them both." She spoke without emotion, like the threat didn't bother her one bit.

Panic spread throughout my body. If what Grace was saying was true, we didn't even have a chance—not unless she took action immediately.

"Why aren't you *doing* something about it?" I shot to my feet. "You have all this knowledge and power, and you're just *sitting* here." I whirled toward the portal behind me. "Let's do something! Let's close it!"

Grace dropped her shoulders. "I'm afraid I can't."

"Can't? Or won't?" I asked with an edge to my tone. "What are you even here for? Why'd you have me wake you if you weren't going to do something about this? You've been distracting everyone with fighting against the Aedes when you *should* be trying to destroy this thing before the realms destroy each other!"

Marek stood beside me. "Ryn is right. We need to do something."

A silent beat passed over the clearing.

"Answer me, Grace!" I shouted.

Grace's soft expression never faltered. "Please. Calm down, and I'll explain."

Anger pulsed through my veins, but I fell silent and waited for her to continue.

"I called out to you in order to stop the portals," Grace said. "But now that I'm here, I've seen the damage your races have caused. The truth is, I've lost my will to fight."

I narrowed my eyes. "I thought you'd been observing all this time. None of this should surprise you."

Grace frowned. "Yes. It's one thing to observe. It's

another to see it firsthand. I am the last Original. I'm…
alone. And I'm not sure I have the heart to restore this
world. The best thing I can do is to distract the Davina and
the Aedes with the war and allow the portal to destroy the
realms."

"*What?*" Allie cried.

She and Kyle were on their feet in less than a second.

"You can't do that!" Kyle objected.

"You're just going to let us die?" I cried.

Grace took a soothing breath. "I believe our essence
will live on as always."

*What a bitch! How can she act so calm when the fate of our
world rested in her hands?*

"Whatever remains of the ashes of our realms will bring
about new life," Grace continued. "Everything will start
fresh. There will be no more war, no more pain and suffering. Everyone will finally be at peace."

My hands balled into fists. "And you just thought you'd
let the rest of us die without any say in the matter? We're
not going to let you do this!"

A hint of amusement crossed Grace's face. "You can't
stop me. Only I have enough power to stop the portal, and
I'm not going to."

"I'll report you to the Davina Council!" I threatened.

Grace's brows shot up. "And you think they'll believe
you? Four teenagers over me, an Original?"

I kept my narrowed gaze on her, but I knew she was
right.

I crossed my arms. "Why tell us, then?"

"Because I want you to stop poking around and asking

so many questions." There was an edge to Grace's voice as she rose to her feet and spread her wings. "You need to accept this is your fate, Ryn. And you need to accept that there's nothing you can do to stop it."

Grace shot into the sky, leaving my friends and me alone at the foot of the portal.

My stomach dropped.

"Wait!" Marek called after her.

Grace continued flying away from us without missing a beat.

"Shit." Marek raked his fingers through his hair. "What are we going to do now?"

Kyle's mouth hung open, like he wanted to give an answer he didn't have.

"Maybe…" Allie started.

We all turned to look at her.

Allie bit her lip. "Maybe there's something to what Grace was saying."

I let out a breath in disbelief. "You can't actually agree with her, can you?"

Allie shrugged. "I don't know. Maybe starting over is what the world needs."

"This isn't a fresh start for any of us!" I shouted. "This is a *death sentence*!"

"I know—" Allie started to say, but I cut her off.

"I'm not ready to die yet," I stated. "Are you?"

Allie averted her gaze. "No."

"What Grace wants to do is wrong," Marek said through clenched teeth. "There are too many innocent people."

"Yeah." Kyle's lips pursed. "It's wrong on so many levels."

I struggled to steady my heavy breathing. "Then there's only one option."

"What's that?" Allie asked curiously.

My jaw tightened. "We go against Grace."

I couldn't believe it'd come down to this. A group of four teenagers had become the world's last hope.

Since Grace wasn't going to do anything to save the earth, we'd have to figure out a way to destroy the portal ourselves.

14

It was late afternoon by the time we returned to my house. I paced around my bedroom, unable to sit still. I could feel my friends' eyes on me.

"Here's what we're going to do." I spoke confidently, but I didn't feel very enthused about my plan. "We're going to find Malcolm."

"No," Marek objected from where he stood near the window.

A skeptical expression crossed Kyle's face. "You want to go *looking* for him after what he did to you? Are you insane?"

"Don't call me that," I snapped. "I'm not insane."

"Kyle's right," Allie protested. "We can't go looking for Malcolm."

"Yeah," Marek agreed. "It's not a smart idea."

I raised my eyebrows. "Do you have a better idea? Because right now, we're desperate."

I glanced between the three of them. They all stared back silently.

"I say we try to come to some sort of peaceful agreement with Malcolm on our own," I suggested. "From there, we can try to get more Davina on our side. We're wasting time fighting the Aedes. We need to stop this fighting and get everyone on common ground. With enough supporters and enough essence, maybe we don't need Grace at all. We could collapse the portal ourselves."

"What if—" Kyle started to say, but I cut him off.

"The least we can do is try." I wasn't taking no for an answer. "The only thing we know for certain is that if we don't try, we—and everyone we love—will die."

Night fell before we landed on the front lawn of Trenton's old house. In the dark, it seemed even more eerie than the first time I was here. The chipping paint, curtained windows, and splintered front door frame screamed *Go Away!* Perhaps in some ways, this house truly was haunted.

I thought it was best if I approached Malcolm alone. Otherwise, he might think it was an ambush. My friends snuck around the side of the house to hide in case I needed them.

My knees shook as I walked toward the front door and reached for the door knob. Before my hand could close around it, a light breeze pushed the door open on its loose hinges, as if inviting me inside.

Freaky.

The hardwood floor creaked under my weight, and a strong dusty scent met my nose. I glanced around the abandoned home, but I couldn't see more than four feet in front of me through the darkness.

"Malcolm?" I called. His name didn't come out as strong and commanding as I intended it to. I cleared my throat and repeated his name.

Only silence returned my call.

I stepped farther into the house and peeked into the kitchen. It was strangely quiet without the hum of the appliances filling the air. I crossed the entrance hall and carefully stepped over the broken vase into the living room.

"Malcolm," I called again. "It's Ryn. I want to talk."

My heart leapt inside my chest as a loud *bang* filled the air, like the sound of a close-range gunshot. I whirled around. My heart slowed when I realized the bang was just a gust of wind slamming the front door into its frame.

I took a deep breath and turned. I practically leapt out of my skin when I rammed into a tall figure cloaked in black. I stumbled back several steps and almost tripped over the coffee table. My pulse quickened at the sight of him.

I expected Malcolm to leap forward and attack me, to lunge for my throat or throw a fireball at my face, but he stood as still as a statue.

My heart rate slowed, and I took a cautious step forward. "Malcolm?"

He lowered his hood. I could just barely make out his expression in the darkness. His lips turned down at the corners, and his shoulders slumped. He looked like the kind of man who'd lost all hope. He put up no fight... almost as if he'd resolved himself to letting me take the first shot.

"What are you doing here?" He made it sound like I was the last person in the world he wanted to see. I probably was.

I cleared my throat. "I want to talk."

"You didn't come here to fight?" He sounded surprised.

"No," I assured him. "I want to negotiate peace. The Aedes will listen to you."

Malcolm frowned. "You think we'll agree to peace after what the Davina did to us? You've killed hundreds of our recruits in the last few days."

"We've lost people, too," I pointed out. "Look, there's something bigger going on here. If we don't do something about it, all of us are going to die."

"What are you talking about?" he demanded.

"The line between the realms is thinning," I explained. "A portal to your realm is opening."

"Yeah," Malcolm said like it was obvious. "That's why Grace has returned, isn't it? She wants to keep the portal closed so we can't return."

"No, she—" I stopped abruptly.

Why hadn't it ever occurred to me that all the Aedes wanted to do was return to a realm they could call their own? Everyone always made it sound like all the Aedes wanted was power and that they wanted to take over the earth.

"Grace was *meant* to keep the portal closed," I told him, "but it's not why you think. The portals themselves are the threat."

Malcolm seemed intrigued. He let me continue.

I explained what Grace had told us earlier, how the realms would destroy each other if we didn't do something about it first. I told him about how Grace had given up and wanted to wash our slates clean, to give birth to a new realm where none of us survived.

"Grace is using you as a distraction," I explained. "If you retreat and stop fighting the Davina in Eagle Valley, then maybe everyone else will see Grace's true colors and we can convince them to help us prevent this."

A hard expression crossed Malcolm's face. "Even if what you're saying is true, peace between our two races will never work. The Davina and the Aedes have never listened to each other. Maybe if Sylvia hadn't left me, she could've convinced them, but now…"

"Maybe the Davina will listen this time if we—"

"You don't get it, do you?" Malcolm exploded. "Your people have made us out to be monsters when all we ever wanted was to survive!"

I froze, momentarily dumbstruck. "Survive?"

"Yes!" Malcolm shouted. "I learned a lot living around Davina for the last two decades. Most Aedes don't get why you hate us so much. The way our stories go, *you're* the power-hungry monsters."

"So—"

"So you think we feed off human essence for fun!" Malcolm roared. "Some abuse their power, but the rest of us only access human essence because it's the only way for us to survive."

Malcolm might as well have dropped a brick on my chest. How could the Davina have had it so wrong all this time? Unless Malcolm was lying to manipulate me...

"You mean... human essence keeps you alive?" I asked.

"Of course it does! We're not immortal. How else would we survive?"

I didn't have a decent answer. I'd assumed because they were direct descendants of the gods, their healing abilities kept them alive until old age. I'd never given it a second thought. I was an idiot.

"We have the unique ability to borrow—access—another being's essence," Malcolm explained.

"So the Davina can't—?"

"No," he answered before I finished the question. "Not modern-day Davina, anyway. The Aedes, however, can borrow essence and transform it into life energy. We use it to grow and stay alive."

"Can't you pull your essence from the earth?" I asked.

"Yes," Malcolm answered. "But it has its limits—for all races. Borrowing essence from another being provides an easier channel than taking from the earth. It allows us to access enough to stay alive."

My jaw hung slack. "Why don't the Davina know about this?"

Malcolm crossed his arms, but his tone softened. "I

suspect some of them do and have decided to keep it from the rest of you. It's a good way to keep you believing we're worth killing."

He couldn't be telling the truth. Was Malcolm really more trustworthy than the Davina Council?

Probably, I thought.

"If the Davina Council knows, why would they let us keep killing you?" I asked.

Malcolm's jaw tensed. "There are Aedes who've given the rest of us a bad name."

Like Clinton, I thought.

"Perhaps the Davina don't realize some of us only take what we need," Malcolm continued. "They lump us all together as monsters and won't entertain the truth."

I don't believe this! Though, the truth was, I believed every word, and it broke my heart.

"This racism has to end," I stated. "The hatred needs to stop."

Malcolm eyed me like I was a poor helpless little girl who just didn't understand. "And I suppose you're going to lead the charge?

I held my head high. "Yes. If I have to."

Malcolm sighed heavily. Obviously, he had no faith in me.

"Why would I help you?" he asked. "You killed my son."

Guilt slammed into my gut at the mention of Trenton.

My gaze dropped to my feet, and my voice came out small. "He was killing my friend. I tried to stop him, but—" My words caught in my throat. "I wouldn't have hurt him if I thought I had any other choice."

Malcolm's lips pressed into a thin line, as if contemplating whether or not to trust me. "How do I know you're not lying?"

I sighed. "Would I be here if I trusted Grace?"

Malcom still looked skeptical.

"We've all had to make sacrifices in this war," I said. "But the fact is, we want the same thing—to survive. And that's not going to happen unless we band together."

Silence momentarily settled over the house.

"All you want from me is to retreat?" he asked.

"Yes," I answered. "We need the Davina to focus on the real issue. They need to know Grace isn't on their side."

Malcolm paused for what felt like a whole minute.

"Okay, I'll give you a chance," he finally said.

Hope soared in my chest.

"But—" Malcolm's word came out harsh, softening my hope. "If you can't convince them of the truth and they attack us again, we will do what we have to in order to defend ourselves."

I nodded. "That's fair. I will do what I can to keep them from attacking your people again."

I didn't know *how* I was going to do that, but one way or another, I would figure it out. If I didn't, time would eventually run out for all of us.

I reached out my hand. "Truce?"

Malcolm hesitated before shaking it. "Truce."

"Where can I find you if I need to contact you again?" I asked.

"Right here," he answered.

I turned to leave, feeling optimistic. As I stepped out the

door, something caught my attention out of the corner of my eye. I did a double take, but the flash of white I'd spotted was gone.

My mouth went dry. I could've sworn I spotted white feathers disappearing around the side of the house—and I wasn't sure those feathers belonged to any of my friends.

15

*M*y opponent grunted as I sank my foot into his gut. What he had in strength, I made up for in speed. His thick arm swung out, reaching for me, but I ducked and threw myself forward. I tackled him to the ground like a football player.

Kyle coughed. "Jesus, Tyler. Where'd you learn to fight like that?"

I offered him my hand and helped him to his feet. I shrugged. "I didn't think I was that good. Maybe don't take it so easy on me next time."

"He wasn't taking it easy on you," a familiar voice said.

I turned to see Marek standing nearby, observing us. I hadn't realized he and Allie had finished sparring.

Yes. Sparring. Again. Like useless maniacs.

A new training schedule had finally been issued, and we'd been *required* to report to the valley for training. All around us, groups of Davina fought one another, but it felt more like we were playing games than actually preparing for anything.

"This is pointless," I complained to Marek. "If Malcolm was being honest with me—and I think he was—we're not going to need to know all this. We *should* be trying to convince everyone we can of the truth."

Fletcher was the first person on that list, but I hadn't seen him all day. We needed to talk to him first. If we couldn't even convince Fletcher, we had no hope of convincing anyone else. When Allie and I went to go find him earlier, one of the councilmembers followed us back to the school. We had to fake using the restroom so they wouldn't get suspicious.

Someone cleared their voice from behind me. "Miss Tyler."

I whirled around to find Anthony Lucas, head of the Davina Council, glaring at me from several feet away. Three other guys in suits stood behind him, like they were the freaking secret service. I recognized Mr. Harris among them.

"Yes? Can I help you?" I tried to sound sweet and innocent, but it didn't really work for me.

"Why don't you and your friends come with us?" Anthony suggested. It sure didn't sound like we had a choice.

All three of my friends came to stand beside me. Marek's shoulder crossed over my own protectively.

"Why?" I demanded.

Anthony cleared his throat and glanced around at the other Davina, like he was afraid I was about to make a scene. I wasn't, unless he gave me a reason. The look he gave me told me he had plenty of reasons.

"We can discuss this further in private," Anthony said.

I crossed my arms. "I'd like to know what I'm getting into first."

Anthony's jaw tightened. "It wasn't a suggestion. You and your friends are to come with us. Now."

It looked as if he was trying to physically restrain himself from dragging me behind him by my hair.

I glanced to Marek. I'd never seen him look so uncertain and scared before.

"We should go with them," Marek said under his breath.

Allie and Kyle both wore the same look Marek did. Reluctantly, I gave in.

I held my shoulders back, trying to appear strong as I followed behind Anthony. The truth was, I was terrified of what he might want.

Anthony and the three secret service guys led us up to the school and into Mrs. Presley's old office. The room wasn't much bigger than my bedroom.

The first thing I noticed was Grace seated behind the large desk near the window. The surface of the desk was empty, like they'd already removed Mrs. Presley's memory from the room.

"Please sit," Grace said sweetly, gesturing to the two seats opposite her.

My friends and I exchanged a wary glance, but eventually, Allie and I claimed the two chairs. Marek stood behind me with his hands on the back of my seat. His knuckles touched my shoulder in a comforting gesture.

Mr. Harris shut the door behind us, and silence settled over the room.

"Is something wrong?" I asked innocently.

Anthony crossed the room to stand next to Grace. He placed his hands on the surface of the desk and leaned toward me. His eyes narrowed, and his lips tightened. "Where were you last night?"

My expression never faltered as I met his stare, but inside, I was screaming. *How do they know?*

Grace had the Davina Council wrapped around her little finger. I wasn't inclined to admit the truth in front of any of them. We needed more time to share the truth with the other Davina before Grace found out what we were up to.

"What do you mean?" I asked, like I had no clue what he was talking about. "I was at home last night, like every night."

"I didn't ask for attitude," Anthony barked.

"But it's the truth." I mean, technically it *was* true. I'd gone home after we met up with Malcolm.

"We know you went to see that scum demon last night," Anthony growled. "What we don't know is *why*."

I leaned back in my chair. "I don't know what you're talking about."

I looked to my friends. They all quickly denied it as well.

Anthony gritted his teeth. "I'm going to ask you one last time. What did Malcolm want?"

I sat up straighter. "And I'm going to tell you again; I don't know what you're talking about."

Anthony let out a heavy breath. Grace just sat there looking content, like she was happy to watch Anthony yell at us.

"You're working with that demon," Anthony accused. "What are you planning?"

Anthony took one quick step around the side of the desk. Before he could get up in my face, Marek stepped between us. Their noses were inches apart.

"She said she doesn't know anything," Marek snarled. "Leave her alone."

Anthony's nostrils flared. "Fine. If *she's* not going to talk, maybe *one* of you will."

One of Anthony's three henchmen lunged for Kyle. Allie shrieked, while I gasped.

"Hey!" Kyle struggled away from the guy. He quickly broke free and straightened his sleeve.

Anthony pushed past Marek and faced Kyle. "Spread your wings."

"What?" Kyle demanded.

Anthony leaned in closer. "Spread. Your. Wings."

Kyle looked to me, then to Allie. I wished I could help him, but what were we going to do? Overpower the most powerful Davina alive and her four trolls?

"Do as he says," Grace instructed.

Kyle stood still for several more seconds before giving in. He pulled his shirt over his head, and large white wings slowly grew from his back.

Anthony reached for Kyle's shoulders and forced him onto his knees. "You have one last chance. What are you planning with Malcolm?"

"Stop!" Marek shouted. "We told you we don't know anything. You must be mistaking us for someone else."

A smirk spread across Anthony's face. "Wrong answer."

In a flash, Anthony ripped a handful of feathers out of Kyle's wings.

Kyle cried out in pain. I winced at the same time Allie's hands slapped in front of her mouth. I thought I even saw Mr. Harris flinch from where he stood in the corner of the room. Marek's fists clenched beside me. I bit down hard on the inside of my lip to keep from spewing insults at the Council.

Allie looked to me with fear in her eyes, begging me to tell the truth.

"Still don't want to talk?" Anthony taunted.

He crossed in front of Kyle, grazing the handful of feathers across his cheek. Kyle turned his face away, and a wild expression entered Anthony's eyes. The Davina Council had officially gone mad trying to win this war.

A moment later, Anthony's fist connected with Kyle's jaw. Blood spurted from Kyle's mouth and across the hardwood floor.

Allie stared down at the blood in horror. When her eyes met Kyle's, he shot back the smallest shake of his head. He didn't want her to speak.

"Tell us!" Anthony thundered a moment before his foot sank into Kyle's groin.

Kyle grunted, and his hands shot between his legs protectively.

Anthony shoved his hand into Kyle's dark hair and

smashed his face against the side of the bookcase near the door.

I yelped. Beside me, Marek's knuckles turned white as his hands curled into tighter fists.

Anthony dragged Kyle upward by his hair and shoved him across the room. Kyle's wing twisted under him when he landed.

Allie shot to her feet. "Let him go!"

Anthony paused. "Are you ready to tell the truth?"

"Yes!" Allie cried. "Just stop!"

Well, shit. We were all going to die.

I quickly cut in before Allie could say more. "You're making a bigger deal out of this than it needs to be! We went to find Malcolm because we wanted to fight him after he kidnapped me. But when we got there…"

Crap. I needed a good lie—and fast.

"When you got there… what?" Anthony prodded.

Marek jumped to my rescue. "He was gone by the time we got to his house."

Anthony narrowed his eyes. "Why didn't you say that to begin with?"

"Because our mentor would be mad at us for trying to deal with him ourselves," I lied. It was the best I could come up with.

Anthony didn't look like he believed me.

"Let them go." Grace's bored voice cut through the momentary silence.

Anthony hesitated. "What?"

"Let them go," she repeated. She never tore her gaze from the window.

It took Anthony another moment, but he finally gave in. "Fine."

Marek rushed to Kyle and helped him to his feet.

"Please return to training with the rest of the Davina," Grace instructed.

I didn't see the point, but I also didn't think we had a choice. I stood and breezed past the councilmembers without making eye contact. I swung the door open and stopped dead in my tracks. Allie nearly rammed into me.

Casey straightened immediately from where she leaned against the wall. Her eyes widened like a deer in the headlights.

"You!" I accused.

Casey took a cautious step back. "Me, what?"

"You turned us in. You followed us last night and tried to get us in trouble!"

It was *her* feathers I'd seen outside Malcolm's. It had to be.

"I don't know what you're talking about," Casey said flatly.

I stared at her in disbelief. I barely noticed Marek drag Kyle past me toward the hospital ward.

"I think you know exactly what I'm talking about," I snapped.

Casey held her hands up in surrender. "Seriously, I'm just waiting for my dad."

"Right," I said with an eye roll. "This is fun for you, isn't it?"

Casey crossed her arms. "No, actually, it's not."

So she was sticking to her story.

"You're such a liar." I lunged for her.

Before I could get my hands on that pretty little face of hers, Allie caught me and dragged me away. I struggled out of her grip, but she dug her fingernails into my arm.

"Stop it, Ryn," Allie hissed. "We have bigger problems than Casey. We need to be on our best behavior."

Allie's words struck me, and I stopped struggling. Allie was right. If the Davina Council figured out that we were trying to make peace with Malcolm, we'd all be killed for treason.

And I was determined to save the world before I died.

16

Training ticked by slowly, but I was able to channel my anger into it and knock a huge Protector on his ass twice. Apparently, I wounded his pride, because he gave up trying to teach me and asked Allie to spar with him instead.

I was relieved when training ended and we were given permission to go home. I still hadn't seen Fletcher all day, so I headed back up to the school to see if he was in his classroom. Marek took my hand and followed, insisting that I shouldn't be left alone.

When we turned down the hall to Fletcher's classroom, I was surprised to see Grace headed our way. I kept my head down, but we didn't make it past her unnoticed. Grace stepped in front of us, blocking our path. She stood with her hands crossed in front of her and a smile on her face.

Shit. What did she want now?

"Ryn," Grace said pleasantly. "Can I have a word with you?"

I glanced to Marek warily. Could I say no to her?

Grace's eyes traveled the length of Marek's body. "Alone?"

I couldn't for the life of me imagine what she wanted to talk about—unless Casey had overheard everything with Malcolm and told Grace the truth. Maybe she wanted to walk me to my execution.

"It's okay," Grace said sweetly.

I didn't trust her.

"Actually, we're kind of busy." I tried to step around her, but Grace blocked my path a second time.

Marek's hand tightened in mine, like he was physically trying to restrain himself from lashing out at Grace.

"I'm sure whatever it is can wait." The way she said it implied anything could wait for *her*, like the pleasure of her company was the most important thing in the world.

I shifted my weight between my feet. "Um…"

"All I want is a moment of your time," Grace pushed. She hadn't dropped the motherly façade. "It'll only take a few minutes."

Marek could no longer contain himself. "She said no."

Grace narrowed her eyes at him.

"It's fine," I cut in before a fight broke out. "We can talk."

Marek looked uncertain, but I squeezed his hand to let him know that I would be all right.

"Anything you say in front of Ryn, you can say in front of me," Marek argued.

Somehow, I knew Grace wasn't going to go for that.

"I'll be okay," I assured him.

Marek's face fell, but I dropped his hand and followed behind Grace.

She led me down the hall and up the stairs. My fingers shook against the railing. What could she possibly want from me?

Grace stepped into Mr. Collins's classroom and shut the door behind us. I glanced around the room cautiously, as if waiting for one of the Davina Council members to jump out and attack me, but we were alone.

I swallowed hard and crossed my arms over my chest. "What did you have to drag me away from my boyfriend for? He was right, you know. Anything you say in front of me can be said in front of him."

Grace walked around the student desks to the front of the room. She leaned against Mr. Collins's desk and pursed her lips. "I want you to tell me the truth of what you were doing at Malcolm's."

Grace's tone came out friendly but stale. She reminded me of my old therapist, who seemed friendly enough, but you knew under that fake smile, she was judging you.

My jaw tensed. "I told you. We went to get revenge. We didn't find it."

Grace's expression remained cold. "We've known each other for a long time, Ryn. I thought by now you could be honest with me."

She might've been watching me my whole life, but I'd only just met Grace. Whatever connection she thought we might have, I didn't feel it.

"If that's all you wanted from me, I think I'll get back to

my boyfriend now." I turned, but before I could twist the doorknob, Grace spoke again.

"I think honesty is best for both of us, Ryn."

I whirled around. "Then why weren't you honest with me to begin with?"

Grace dropped her head. Holy crap. Had I made her feel bad?

"Perhaps I can make up for it," she said.

"How?" I was actually curious to know the answer.

Grace took a long, deep breath. "Would you like to know what really happened to your father?"

What did she just say?

Her offer struck me like a punch to the gut. My breath stalled. I wasn't sure if it was out of fear or excitement. I hesitated. Grace couldn't actually know what happened to my dad, could she? She was only saying it to keep me here —for whatever reason. Then again, Grace had been observing the world all this time. It was possible she knew much more about what happened in our world than she let on.

"You actually know what happened to him?" I asked, my voice low.

Grace nodded. "Take a seat."

I stepped closer to the desk she'd gestured to.

"It's a long story," she said, like that would make me feel better about accepting her invitation to sit.

I sank into the chair. "What do you know about him?"

"There's a reason I chose you to wake me, Ryn."

"Because of my father?" I asked.

She dropped her gaze. "Because of your father's mistake… and mine."

What could she possibly mean by that?

"Before I chose you," Grace explained, "I chose your father."

I gasped. This couldn't be real. *Grace is lying to me.*

"The line between the realms has been thinning for many years," she told me. "I led your father to Eagle Valley, but I made the mistake of leading him to the site of the portal before he could wake me. He must've felt my urgency in reaching it because it was close to finally opening fully. Then your father learned he was about to have a child."

Me. And then, poof, he was gone.

"He became desperate," Grace continued. "But he hadn't found me yet. Communicating with him—as you're very familiar with—was difficult."

You can say that again.

"Unlike you," Grace said, "he knew he'd been chosen because he grew up hearing the stories of my powers. He knew he was running out of time. To save you—and the rest of the world—he tried to use my powers on his own. However, a mortal like your father was unable to access all of my powers at once. He couldn't collapse the portal by himself. But he didn't give up. Your father threw himself into the portal with a portion of my essence."

A lump grew in my throat. Could this be true? Or was she just telling me what I wanted to hear?

More than anything, I wanted it to be true. It meant that my father had died a hero. He hadn't walked out on us because he didn't want me. He wanted me so much that he sacrificed himself to save me.

Grace cleared her throat. "The portal partially collapsed, but it only delayed the threat. The same portal your father sacrificed himself to eighteen years ago has been rebuilding itself. I spent many years searching for a new Davina to share my powers with. I had to be selective so that I could build a connection with whoever I chose. That way, they could find me first, instead of the portal. I searched many years for the perfect person, but I kept coming back to you."

"Because of my strange essence?" I asked.

Grace's brow furrowed. "Your essence? No. You were only a child, but already, I could see that you had a good heart. You couldn't be manipulated by the Aedes as others could."

I thought of Clinton and how he'd manipulated my mom but never manipulated me.

"The more I thought about it, the more I realized that perhaps choosing a child was the best option," she said. "It would allow us to grow a stronger connection so I could lead you to me."

And our connection had still sucked. But then again, I *had* found her before it was too late. But it was too late for my father…

"So you're the reason my dad's dead?" My voice cracked.

"I—" Grace paused a moment, as if carefully considering how to word her answer. "Your father acted by himself."

My fingers tightened around the corner of the desk until my knuckles turned white. "And he'd still be alive if you hadn't chosen him and messed up!"

"Ryn, I—"

"Unless… unless he's still alive…" I thought out loud.

Grace shook her head. "No, he's gone."

"How can you know?" I bit back. "Maybe he made it to the other side. Or maybe he's trapped inside the portal."

"It's not possible," Grace insisted.

I shot to my feet. "You don't know that for sure! You never tried to save him, did you?"

The portal was opening again. If he survived, maybe I had a chance to save him. I'd never know until I tried.

"Ryn," Grace started, but I didn't listen.

I whirled around and raced out of the room.

I didn't care if it was a long shot. I had to save my father.

I sprinted down the hall and descended the stairs to the front of the building. Footsteps followed behind me, but I pushed forward. My fingers just barely grazed the door handle when strong hands grabbed my biceps and spun me around.

"Ryn, what's wrong?" Marek's voice filled with alarm.

"My dad—Grace said—there's a chance—" I sputtered between heavy breaths.

"Slow down," Marek demanded.

The words spilled out of me. "Grace said my dad went into the portal. What if he's still in there, Marek?"

I didn't give him a chance to respond. I spun back toward the door and raced outside. Before my feet touched the grass, wings had sprouted from my back. I flapped them hard and launched myself into the sky. Cold wind rushed by my face, tangling my hair into a giant knot.

Marek followed closely behind. Up here, he didn't have a chance to ask any more questions.

The flight to the portal seemed to take hours. My father had encountered the portal almost two decades ago, but it felt like if I didn't get there now, I'd miss my chance at saving him.

I landed in the grassy clearing with a hard *thud* and stumbled forward. My heart pounded, and I inhaled deep breaths as I approached the portal. The ripples in the air were bigger and more prominent today. The portal was getting stronger.

"Ryn," Marek said softly, as if afraid he might startle me. His fingers grazed across mine, but I barely felt them.

"Dad?" I projected my voice into the rippling air.

Nothing met my ears but the light breeze passing through the trees.

"Dad, are you there? It's your daughter, Kathryn."

No response.

I realized that if my dad had survived the portal, he wouldn't even know my name. How freaking sad was that?

"Daniel," I tried instead. "I'm Gloria Tyler's daughter! I'm here to help."

Seconds ticked by. I waited for a strong, deep voice to call out from within the portal—the voice I'd always imagined.

The weight of Marek's hand settled on my shoulder. "Ryn, I don't think he's—"

"He could be!" I snapped my head in Marek's direction. "We don't know what it's like inside the portal or on the other side! He could've survived."

Marek bit his lower lip, like he wanted to say more but was trying to restrain himself.

I turned my gaze back to the portal. I had to believe my dad was still there. All I ever wanted was to hear an explanation, to reunite with him. I wanted him to tell me he didn't leave because he didn't want me but because he had to, that he thought of me every day since and regretted that he never had a chance to tell me he loved me.

"Maybe he can't hear us," I theorized.

I stepped closer to the portal. Marek's arm wrapped around my waist, holding me back.

"Don't touch it." A hint of alarm entered his tone.

I pushed his protective arm away from me. "Why not? If he's in there—"

"If he's in there, it means you could get stuck in there, too."

"So, what do we do?" I asked desperately.

My eyes darted across the portal in search of a weak spot. If we could somehow widen the portal, perhaps my father could find his way out.

Before Marek had a chance to stop me, I conjured a white fireball and hurled it at the center of the ripple. My essence passed through the rippling air, like it'd been swallowed up. Then it expanded like an explosion, as if there was an invisible brick wall just behind the rippling air.

"Dad!" I yelled again.

Silence.

My blood began to boil the longer we waited. Tension grew in my head. I drew my arm back to throw another fireball.

"Ryn." Marek's voice stopped me. "You could end up doing more harm than good."

"We have to try something!" I cried.

I sent another ball of essence into the portal. It did nothing but expand rapidly like the last one had.

"Help me, Marek!" I begged.

Marek opened his mouth but only sighed. Finally, he spoke in a whisper. "I don't know what to do."

"Don't just stand there! Do something!" My hands shook at my sides as the urge to punch something—anything—overcame me. I shot another fireball at the portal, and then another and another.

Marek just stood there watching me freak out. An expression of hopelessness settled on his face.

Help me! I wanted to scream.

I reached out a hand to plunge it into the portal, but my fingers just barely grazed the center ripple before Marek grabbed my elbow and whirled me around. I struggled away from him, wanting nothing more than to dive into the portal to save my dad. Marek only caught my wrists and restrained me tighter.

"Let go of me!" I objected.

"Please, stop." The look in his eyes begged me to comply. "You're going to hurt yourself."

My bottom lip quivered.

Say something more, I thought. *Tell me he's in there. Tell me we can save him. Please let me go so I can save him.*

But I realized Marek was right. There was nothing more I could do.

I sank to my knees and bit the inside of my cheek. A tear rolled down my face and fell into the grass. Marek knelt behind me and pulled me into his arms.

"He's really gone, isn't he?" My voice cracked, and I squeezed my eyes shut.

This wasn't right. All this time, I thought my dad might be dead, but I wasn't sure I actually believed it until now.

"There's no saving him, is there?" I sobbed.

Marek buried his face in my hair and kissed the top of my head. "I'm so sorry, Ryn."

I covered my face with my hands. "How can Grace do this? My dad sacrificed himself to save the world, and now she's just going to let it end. She has no right to do this. It's her fault my dad is gone. It's her fault for everything."

My shoulders heaved uncontrollably. I didn't want to cry here in front of Marek, but that thought only caused me to sob harder.

"Grace isn't going to let this portal destroy the world," Marek said. "I won't let her do it."

I drew away from Marek to look him in the eyes. "You won't?"

"I won't," he emphasized. "I am *not* going to let your father's death be in vain."

Fresh tears rolled down my cheeks as a new wave of emotions overcame me. Marek's strong arms wrapped around me again. I pressed my face into his bare chest and stayed wrapped in his arms until my tears dried and the sun set.

I was on the verge of falling asleep and couldn't find the strength to stand. I would stay out here under the stars in his arms all night if I had to. I just didn't want to move. It would only make all of this too real and remind me of the heartbreaking truth.

Eventually, Marek rose to his feet, cradling me in his arms. I clung to him, but he didn't say anything as he launched us both into the sky and flew me home.

Marek landed softly on my front lawn and carried me up the front steps. The porch swing swayed beneath me as he set me down. I blinked my eyes open to look at him. The porch light created a halo around his head, but his face was cast in shadows.

"Thank you for bringing me home," I whispered.

He bent to push my hair from my face. "It's what I'm here for."

I struggled to sit up. Somehow, my high emotions had translated into physical pain in my muscles.

"I should probably get inside," I said. "I'll see you tomorrow."

I stood and wrapped him in a hug. All I wanted was to invite him inside and spend the night in his arms, but I knew it'd be wrong to ask. I'd been in enough trouble these past few days with my mom. I held onto Marek a minute longer and then peeled my body off his and said goodbye. It broke my heart to step inside the house without him.

"Kathryn?" Mom called from the kitchen.

I didn't want to face her, but I didn't want to fight, either. I headed down the hall and stopped in the kitchen doorway. "Yeah?"

Mom looked up from the sink, where she was rinsing a bowl after the dinner I missed. I could only imagine what sort of mess I looked like. I was sure my hair was disheveled from flying and my eyes were still red and puffy from crying.

"Kathryn, what's wrong?" She sounded genuinely concerned.

Lie to her, I thought. Mom didn't need to be dragged into this. Then again, it wasn't fair for me to keep this a secret, either.

"It's Davina stuff again, isn't it?" She turned off the faucet and turned to me. "Are you ever going to tell me what's really been going on? The lady at the bank says people are talking about giant birds and angel sightings. I thought it was all supposed to be a secret."

It is, I wanted to say. *But no one cares anymore because our world is colliding with another realm, and they'll inevitably collapse in on each other. What do secrets matter anymore?*

Somehow, I couldn't bring myself to share *that* secret with her. I wasn't sure I was going to say anything, but she continued to stare at me. I knew she wouldn't let me leave without some sort of explanation.

My throat tightened, and tension grew in the air. I was surprised to hear my quiet voice break the silence. "I know what happened to my father."

Mom gasped. "What—how?"

"Maybe we should sit down," I suggested.

Mom's hand gripped the back of the nearest chair to steady herself. After a moment to digest what I'd just said, she sank into it. I sat across from her at the table.

"You can't know what happened to him," she stated.

It wasn't that she didn't believe me. It sounded more like she didn't *want* to believe me, like she was afraid of what I might tell her.

I cleared my throat. "I think it's pretty obvious by now that my dad was a Davina."

Mom nodded.

"Well, he was involved in this war," I said. "Another Davina knew him, and she told me…"

I lifted my gaze to meet my mother's. Her fear was clouded with an expression of hope. She was finally going to get an answer to the one question that had plagued her all these years.

I didn't know how much I could tell her without devastating her beyond belief. How would she feel if she knew like I did that my father's sacrifice had been in vain?

I settled for the easiest explanation. "He sacrificed himself for a lot of people. He didn't leave because of you or because he didn't want me. He left to save us. He was very brave."

I didn't know what I expected from her—perhaps an outburst or for her to call me a liar—but she just sat there.

Mom bit her lower lip. Her voice came out so gentle that it didn't sound like her own. "Can't you see this is why I worry about you, Kathryn? I already lost your father to a Davina battle. I don't want to lose you, too."

I didn't bother correcting her, that he hadn't died in battle, nor could I deny that she might lose me, too. I simply didn't speak. It was easier that way.

"Thank you for telling me," Mom said.

It was strange to hear her talk so softly. Usually, all we did was yell at each other.

"You're glad I told you?" I asked.

Mom thought about it for a moment and then wiped at her eyes. She nodded. "Yeah."

"Mom, I'm sorry—" I started.

"No," she replied with a sniffle. "It's okay. It's good to finally know. I—I think I'm going to go to bed early."

Mom stood and exited the kitchen before I could say anything more. I thought about following her upstairs to comfort her, but I decided to give her space.

I rose from my chair and poured myself a bowl of cereal. It was hard to eat when I didn't have much of an appetite lately. After I finished, I left my dirty dishes in the sink and climbed the stairs.

The door to my mom's bedroom creaked when I peeked my head inside to check on her. She didn't stir as the light from the hallway crossed her bed. Seeing that she was okay, I shut the door and turned to my own bedroom.

I lay in bed and stared up at the ceiling. Since my phone was broken, I didn't have a clock next to me to check the time. No matter how hard I tried to fall asleep, I kept tossing and turning.

After what felt like hours, I kicked back the covers. I wrapped a robe around my body for warmth and tiptoed down the hall. Downstairs, I checked the clock above the

TV. Only an hour had passed since I'd gone to bed. Why did it feel as if time was slowing down?

I was careful to not make any noise when I opened the front door and stepped out onto the porch. I sat on the lowest step and stared up into the sky while I held onto Marek's feather that hung around my neck. The nearby street lamp drowned out most of the stars, but I could still make out the brightest ones. I inhaled deeply and released the tension in my shoulders while I counted each star I could see. I knew I might not have much longer to enjoy all of this.

I was so preoccupied with staring up at the stars that I didn't notice a figure approaching from down the street. I only saw her when she started up the sidewalk toward my house. At first, I couldn't see who it was. Instinct told me to hurry to my feet and lock myself inside. Then a familiar voice came past the shadows.

"Hey, Ryn."

"Casey?" I pulled my robe tighter around me. "What are you doing here?"

Was she here to pick another fight? Something in the cautious way she approached me told me that wasn't the case.

"I was just out walking." I heard the lie in her voice.

"Really?" I eyed her skeptically.

"Okay," she caved. "I came to see you. Mind if I sit?"

I shook my head. As much as I hated Casey, I honestly didn't mind. I actually preferred her company over the empty step beside me. I caught a whiff of Casey's floral perfume as she sat next to me.

"Anyway, I saw you out here and thought…" She trailed off.

"Thought what?"

She shrugged. "It just looked like maybe you could use someone to talk to."

I raised my eyebrows. "And you thought you'd be the perfect person?"

Casey held her hands up in surrender. "Hey, if you don't want me around, I'll leave." She got to her feet.

"No," I said. "Stay."

Casey relaxed back onto the step. Neither of us said anything. But this was Casey. What was I supposed to say to her besides *'Get off my damn lawn'*?

"I hope you don't mind me being so forward about this," Casey said, "but I have to ask… What *happened* earlier?"

I frowned when I looked at her. "You really don't know?"

Innocence crossed her face. "I know you think I turned you in to the Davina Council for something, but you should know that I didn't."

I wasn't sure I believed Casey. If she hadn't followed us to Malcolm's and ratted us out, who did?

"Something big is going on here, isn't it?" Casey asked. "Something bigger than our recent battles with the demons."

"Believe me," I said, "you don't want to know."

"I heard part of the conversation earlier," Casey blurted. "You went to see Trenton's dad?"

My cheeks heated. "Why do you care?"

Casey paused for a moment, like she wasn't quite sure of the answer. "Because I want to help."

Casey sounded honest, like she'd be willing to go against the Davina Council and Grace with us if it meant doing the right thing. But still, it was *Casey*.

My brow furrowed. "You want to help *me*? I thought you'd be more willing to help the Davina Council fight their war."

Casey scoffed. "My dad is Eagle Valley's rep. He hardly wants me in Eagle Valley right now with things the way they are. He's not exactly interested in my help."

I could hear the disappointment in her voice.

A brief silence settled between us before I changed the subject. "Can I ask you something?"

"Sure, but I might not answer," Casey said with a light laugh.

I'd been burning with this question for days. "Did you know what Trenton was?"

Casey lips turned down. She definitely didn't like the question. "You mean, did I know he was half-demon? No, I had no clue. The whole thing… It feels like a betrayal."

I twisted the fabric of my robe in my hands. "You two were close, weren't you?"

Trenton had hinted that they'd been a little more than friends at one point or another.

Casey nodded. "It's hard not to get attached to your training partners. I just can't believe Trenton and Troy are both gone."

"I'm sorry," I whispered. I'd forgotten she'd lost so many people close to her.

Casey shook her head, like I shouldn't be sorry. "I just can't get what you said to me out of my head."

Confusion crossed my face. "What do you mean? What did I say?"

Casey shifted to face me. "You said that one day we'd be fighting together, and we'd be keeping score with how many people we lose. You counted Trenton as the first one lost."

I swallowed hard. I'd been in a state of high emotions when I'd said that. "I didn't mean—"

"You were right," Casey interrupted. "We've lost so many people recently, and that's more important than my petty drama."

I was shocked to hear her admit it. I always thought she had too much pride to ever say she was wrong.

"What's with the drama in the first place?" I asked. "I mean, why do you hate me?"

Casey laughed, like it was a long story she didn't want to get into, but she answered anyway. "You have everything I want."

"*What?*" I had nothing. I didn't have a real home or a father. Hell, I didn't even have half the boobs she had.

"You have Allie, and we used to be best friends," Casey pointed out. "And you have Marek. I always thought that we'd eventually end up together, but then you came along. I don't even have a chance anymore."

Good, I thought. *Marek's mine.*

"I'm going to be honest with you," Casey continued. "I'm a little jealous of how everyone fawned over you when school started. *I* used to be the center of attention at Galen."

I blushed, but I hoped she couldn't see it through the darkness. "People did not *fawn* over me."

"Maybe not to your face, but they sure talked about you a lot."

"What?" I squeaked. "I'm not even interesting."

Casey rolled her eyes. "Tell that to all the guys constantly checking out your ass."

I laughed. "Please. You're the one with the ass worth looking at."

Casey held back a smile. "True."

Silence filled the air between us, but I was surprised to find that it wasn't awkward. I felt almost comfortable sitting next to Casey with no obligation to speak up.

Casey eventually broke the silence. "So, you're not going to tell me what's really happening?"

I bit my lower lip. "Depends. Who sent you here to coerce an answer out of me? Grace? Your dad?"

"No one," she answered like she was offended by the accusation. "I swear."

I couldn't deny the honesty laced in Casey's tone. She was telling the truth. My internal bitch that hated Casey screamed for me to keep my mouth shut, to keep Casey in the dark.

But the rational part of me told me that if she was willing to side with us, she deserved to know the truth. The more Davina we got on our side, the better.

"Okay," I caved. "I'll tell you."

And I did. I told Casey about the portal and how Grace

had given up hope and wanted to let the realms destroy each other. I told her the truth about why we'd gone to visit Malcolm and that we couldn't tell the Davina Council of our peace treaty before we had a chance to convince others of the truth.

"Why haven't you told everyone else yet?" Casey asked curiously.

I frowned. "Most of them will side with Grace no matter what she says. I don't want her locking me up before I have a chance to convince at least a few people of the truth."

"We have to destroy that portal," Casey stated. "No matter what it takes."

Finally, someone understood.

"I know," I said, "but Grace is the only one with enough power, and if she isn't willing to help—"

"Then we'll find another way." Casey sounded like she truly believed we could.

I smiled half-heartedly. It was hard to believe Casey was taking my side.

"Whatever we have to do," Casey said, "I'll stand behind you. I'm not going out of this world without a fight."

My jaw tightened. "Neither am I."

19

I woke early the next morning and rushed through a shower and breakfast before flying to Galen. Dawn was only just breaking, and the streets were quiet.

After talking with Casey last night, I came up with two options. The first was to convince Grace to help us, no matter what it took.

The second… well, I didn't want to think about that.

I soared over the mansion, and my eyes landed on a figure sitting on Galen's rooftop. Her massive white wings were spread out on either side of her, and she had her knees pulled to her chest.

Grace didn't look up when I landed beside her. She continued staring out toward the horizon, like she never heard me.

"Hello, Ryn," she said in a cold voice.

She didn't seem upset to see me. It was more like she was upset that the world hadn't collapsed yet.

I approached her slowly. "Mind if I sit?"

"Go ahead." She sounded like she didn't care either way.

The shingles were rough on my hands as I lowered myself beside her. "What are you doing?"

Grace waited a breath to answer. "Watching the sunrise. I'm not sure how many more we'll have."

I stared out toward the horizon with her. The sun was just beginning to peek up over the trees, casting a yellow glow across the sky.

"You have a thing for nature, don't you?" I asked.

Grace nodded lightly. "Being asleep all this time, I've missed it. You don't realize how much you miss the sun on your skin until it's gone."

I wrapped my arms around my knees and spoke softly. "Then why don't you want to save it?"

Grace finally pulled her gaze off the sky and looked at me. "I think it's time for a fresh start."

"For you, or for all of us?"

My words hung in the air. I didn't mean for the accusation to come out like a slap across the face. I was honestly curious to know what she was feeling. I had to understand her before I could change her mind.

"I don't expect you to understand," Grace finally said.

"I can try," I offered.

Grace pressed her lips together, as if fighting a harsh internal battle. She sighed heavily. "I was in love once."

What? When? I wanted to say, but I kept my mouth shut. I wasn't about to interrupt her.

"After the Davina created humans, we lived with them for many, many years. I fell in love with one of them."

Grace swallowed hard. "We had children together, but neither him nor my children shared my immortality. I had to watch everyone I loved age and die."

My heart broke for her. I couldn't imagine losing Marek the way she lost her husband.

"I stayed behind as long as I could to watch my grandchildren and my great grandchildren grow," Grace continued. "But I couldn't keep watching them die while I continued to live. Many Davina had already returned to Vehena by then. But, by the time I was ready to go, only sixteen of us remained."

A lump rose in my throat. "Do you think Vehena is still out there somewhere?"

Grace shook her head. "I don't think our realm survived."

"And the Aedes realm?" I questioned.

She cleared her throat. "We begged the Aedes to return. We forced those who didn't comply, but obviously, some of them remained. We sealed off their realm. We feared the earth would die if they remained connected. Without the gods' powers to stabilize the realms they created, it just wasn't possible for them to naturally coexist."

"Then what happened?" I was completely engrossed in her story now.

"We watched over the world while we rested. The whole time, I thought I could save it again, but now…"

"Now?" I pressed.

Grace frowned. "Now that I've been awakened, I see how terrible it's truly become. There are so many people suffering. I've seen war after war break out. I've watched humans wipe out entire populations. It's so much worse seeing the cost of war up close. Not to mention poverty, abuse, rape… There's so much cruelty in this world."

I carefully considered Grace's words. She was right about this world being cruel. But she had to believe the world had more to offer.

Grace let out a long breath. "It wasn't always like this. The world used to be good. People actually cared about each other."

"And that's why you want to destroy it?" I asked lightly.

"Yes," she whispered. "I'm the last Original left, and I'm not sure I can do this alone."

"You're not alone, Grace," I pointed out.

She looked at me with uncertainty.

"You have the rest of the Davina behind you."

She dropped her gaze. "It's not the same."

Sympathy filled my heart. "Maybe if you try, you'll find more of what you've been missing."

Grace tilted her head in question. "What do you mean?"

I gestured to the horizon. "You missed the sunrise, and here you are, enjoying it. There are other wonderful things in this world that aren't worth giving up."

"Like?" She sounded skeptical.

"Like community, music, and art," I answered. "Like compassion and joy and love. As long as love still exists in our world, we can survive the rest of the bad stuff together."

The corners of Grace's lips turned down. I still hadn't convinced her.

"Don't give up, Grace," I begged. "There's still good in

the people around us. You have the power to inspire and bring out the best in people. The world needs you, and even though it's hard, I believe you can make it a better place. You can show us how things used to be and teach us so much. Maybe our fresh start doesn't begin with death. Maybe it starts with *you*."

She had to believe this was possible.

"You really think I can be this world's new beginning?" Grace asked.

I nodded. "I really do."

"But—"

"You can't doubt yourself, Grace," I interrupted. "This will only work if you believe in yourself."

Damn. Where was all this wisdom coming from?

Silence stretched between us for what felt like a full minute.

"You must believe there's still good in this world," I stated. "You mentioned the sunshine. Can't you think of at least one more thing?"

Grace contemplated my question for a moment. "I—I guess… laughter."

I smiled, and a small laugh escaped my lips. "Laughter's great. See? There's plenty of beauty in the world if you just look."

Grace bit her lip. "I haven't laughed since I last saw my family."

"Family is another wonderful thing to be grateful for," I pointed out. "Think of all the other families out there, watching the sunrise and laughing together."

Grace nodded.

"If you can't do it for us," I said, "do it for your family. Help us restore the world that was once their home."

Another stretch of silence followed.

Finally, Grace sighed. "Maybe there *are* some things in this world worth saving."

I'm getting through to her!

"Maybe…" Grace paused. "Maybe we *can* set things right again."

"Really?" I couldn't contain my excitement. "You'll help us, then?"

Grace smiled. "I'll help. For my family."

I squealed and leapt to my feet.

Grace stood and held her head high. "I will bring the Davina hope. Once the Davina arrive for training this morning, I will lead them to the portal so they can witness me close it."

Grace is going to help us! I felt more optimistic than I had in a long time.

I only hoped it wasn't too late.

My eyes scanned the clearing. There were so many Davina that some had to stand back in the trees. The crowd buzzed in curiosity. Davina stood on their toes and craned their necks to get a better look at the portal in front of us.

Marek placed his arm around my shoulder, and I leaned into him. Allie and Kyle stood beside us. Next to them, Fletcher stared at the rippling in the air in wonder. Nearby, Casey shot me a smile. Hope surged in my chest.

"Davina!" Grace called.

The clearing quieted.

"I have led you here today to reveal the truth. You have all heard the stories of the portals and know that danger would come to you if one opened." Grace gestured to the rippling air behind her. "This is a tear between the realms, a place in space where the earth and Malum have collided. Each passing day, the portal grows wider. *This* is what I have returned to protect you from."

Whispers spread throughout the crowd.

Can you believe it?

How long has it been here?

She's going to save us!

"What you don't know is the truth about *why* this portal threatens your home," Grace continued. "You fear a portal to Malum because you fear the Aedes on the other side. The truth is, the realms themselves have the power to destroy each other."

A woman gasped behind me.

Grace continued her story, repeating what she'd told me about the Originals losing their home. She went on to tell the Davina about how they pushed the Aedes back to Malum and how they'd been protecting our realm ever since.

"And now," Grace said with her head held high, "I must sever this connection between the realms. I have brought you together to witness this historic event so that you can tell your children and your children's children that the Davina are the hope in this world. The Davina will live to see another day, and together, we will heal this world!"

Applause spread across the clearing. For the first time, I joined in on it.

Grace slowly spun toward the portal, and the crowd fell silent. My heart pounded in excitement, and sweat rose to my skin. The moment we'd all been waiting for was finally here. I couldn't believe I was a part of it.

Grace took a deep breath to collect herself. A moment later, purple essence shot from her hands. It was even more fantastic than the first time I saw it. Purple waves of essence danced across her skin and lit up her body as if she was made of electricity. She directed the essence in a massive stream straight into the portal. Her essence expanded inside of it, and the clearing became cast in a purple tint. It was so bright that I had to tear my gaze away from the portal. I looked to Marek instead.

Above us, the clouds darkened, and a crack of thunder vibrated throughout the clearing. I cursed under my breath.

"What?" Marek gazed down at me.

"A thunderstorm, right now?" I said.

Marek nodded toward Grace. "Can't you tell? Grace is doing it. Controlling the weather is one of the powers of the Originals."

My disappointment quickly turned to wonder. Suddenly, a thunderstorm didn't seem at all like a bad thing.

"I didn't know that." I almost had to shout to be heard over the wind that had picked up.

Leaves began to break off the trees, and I had to gather my hair at the nape of my neck to keep it from tangling. Marek rubbed his warm hand up and down my arm to help ward off the chill brought on by the strong winds. The portal changed from rippling to swirling.

This is it, I told myself. I rose to my toes to look over the shoulder of the Davina in front of me. *This is the moment we make history.*

In the blink of an eye, a lightning bolt came down from the sky and struck the portal. Before I could truly process it, the air expanded around us rapidly and slammed into my chest. The force blasted my body backward into the Davina behind me.

I gasped for breath and stared up at the sky. The dark clouds began to lighten.

Finally, the air returned to my lungs, and I sat up.

All around me, Davina had been knocked off their feet. Confusion crossed everyone's faces as they tried to piece together the events of the last few seconds. Had Grace done it? Had the portal been destroyed?

I looked back toward Grace, but my heart immediately sank. I expected the air to be clear where the portal once stood.

Instead, the rippling was more prominent than ever.

Grace propped herself up on her elbows. From where I lay in the grass, I could see the look on her face. Her eyes widened in horror as she stared at the air in front of her. Grace knew as well as I did that she hadn't destroyed it at all. She'd only widened it.

Our end was about to come sooner than we thought.

I rose to my feet and hurried over to Grace.

"Are you okay? What happened?" I asked in a rush.

Grace's eyes flickered between mine and the portal. She opened her mouth to speak, then closed it.

"Are you hurt?" I asked, frantically searching for any signs of injury.

Grace shook her head, but her eyes remained wide. "I— I waited too long. The portal is too powerful."

I helped her to her feet. "We can still fix this, can't we? Tell me we can save everyone."

The answer I dreaded fell from Grace's lips. "There is nothing we can do."

"But—" My throat felt like it was lined with sandpaper as it closed up around my words.

"I'm sorry," Grace whispered. "I let everyone down. I'm not the hero they thought I was. I am alone now without the other Originals' help. I am powerless to close this portal."

I felt the blood drain from my face.

Grace turned back toward the crowd of Davina. They were all getting to their feet now. She paused, as if the words were too painful to speak, but she pushed on... because she knew she had to.

Grace projected her voice into the crowd. "Please forgive me, Davina."

Tension grew in my jaw. This couldn't be it. Were we truly hopeless?

"You can try again," I encouraged.

Grace shook her head and spoke so only I could hear. "That was all my power."

It was true. We *were* hopeless. Grace had tried her hardest. And it wasn't enough.

"Try again!" I cried, desperately glancing between Grace and the portal.

Grace turned back to the crowd, like she hadn't heard me. "Our final hours have come. It's only a matter of time before this portal breaks open completely and your realm is destroyed. There's nothing more we can do. You should return home and say goodbye to your loved ones."

Murmurs spread across the crowd.

"No! Grace!" I screamed, but she ignored me.

People began moving, pushing other Davina out of the way. Screams filled the air as people were knocked to the ground. Others spread their wings and shot into the sky.

I paused to take in the chaos. Then the reality of what was truly happening sank in. I rushed over to Marek, but the crowd was in a panic. Someone rammed into me, and I fell to the ground.

"Marek!" I screamed. I could no longer see him through the crowd.

Strong hands gripped my arms and pulled me to my feet. I pushed away from whoever had ahold of me until I turned and saw it was Marek. I flung my arms around his neck.

"This can't be happening," I cried into his shoulder.

Marek wrapped me in a protective hug. "I can't believe it, either."

Allie and Kyle pushed through the panicked crowd and found us. I kept one arm around Marek's neck and placed the other over Allie's shoulder, pulling her in to me. Kyle wrapped an arm around her, and my friends and I joined in a group hug.

Davina continued to rush out of the clearing until we were the only group left.

Fletcher approached slowly. I dropped my hands from Marek and Allie. I didn't see Grace anywhere.

Fletcher's gaze dropped to the grass. "I'm sorry. I was wrong not to listen to you, Ryn. I put all my faith in Grace, and… and this happened."

Allie bit her lower lip. "Now what do we do?"

"We do as Grace said," Fletcher replied, as if he'd given up hope. "We say goodbye and enjoy what time we have left."

"There has to be *something* we can do," I insisted. "Grace could've tried harder!"

Fletcher shook his head. "I'm not sure if she could've. She used a lot of power, and it didn't work."

I wouldn't give up yet... not until I breathed my last breath.

There must be another way, I thought. The longer I stared at the portal, the more the conversation around me faded.

Eventually, the sound of Allie's voice calling my name pulled me from my thoughts. "Ryn. It's time to go."

"Actually," I replied, never taking my eyes off the portal. "I... I'd kind of like to be alone right now."

"Ryn." Marek sounded hurt. He reached out to take my hand.

I finally looked at him. "I'll be back to say goodbye," I promised.

Marek's expression softened. "Are you sure?"

"Yeah." I nodded.

My friends glanced between each other, like they weren't convinced it was safe to leave me alone. I didn't give them any other choice.

"I'll be fine," I assured them. "You guys go have fun. I'll be there soon."

"Come on," Marek encouraged my friends. "She has someone else to say goodbye to."

It occurred to me that Marek thought I wanted to stay to say goodbye to my dad.

My eyes followed my friends as they took flight. I waited until they were out of view before I turned back toward the portal. I stepped toward it cautiously.

A strange tingling filled my body and spread across my skin. It was the same kind of magic I felt when I was defending myself from Malcolm. I stopped just feet from the portal and focused on the new energy flowing through my body.

What was this strange feeling? Why hadn't anyone mentioned it before when they told me about essence?

Maybe because none of them had experienced it before. Maybe because, like Grace, I was different for some reason. I just didn't know why.

I closed my eyes and focused on this energy and brought it to the surface. When I felt it reach my fingertips, I finally peeled my eyes open. White mist rose out of my palm and swirled in the air above my hand.

I pictured the smoky essence forming into an orb like the fireballs I was so used to conjuring. To my surprise, the magic complied with my demands. In that moment, I realized I could direct and control this new essence.

I aimed my palms toward the ground and directed the essence away from me. It stretched out of my hands like a ghostly snake and slithered a foot above the ground. My eyes followed the wispy magic in awe, as if I wasn't the one controlling it.

I wasn't sure what I was doing when I sent the magic to wrap itself around the portal. It spread out above the portal like a force field. Through the strange fog, I saw the rippling in the air pause for a moment, but it was back a second later, as though the portal was flickering on and off.

Could this new, unexplored essence be the answer to saving us all?

It seems too easy.

Just as the thought crossed my mind, a powerful wave shot me backward. My body flew into the air, and I landed on my ass a good fifteen feet from the portal.

I cursed and rolled over, rubbing my tailbone. Finally, I lifted my gaze only to see that I hadn't done a damn thing to destroy the portal. The air rippling across the clearing continued.

But I had done something, I thought. The portal had flickered under the power of my essence.

This new essence couldn't help us like this, but maybe it could help us in another way. There was only one option left.

That can't be the only answer, I thought.

But it was. We'd run out of time.

My chest compressed, and my legs shook. Hot tears rushed from my eyes and fell into the grass. My fingers sank into the dirt as I curled my hands into tight fists and ripped the grass roots from the earth. It didn't help stifle the agony ripping through me.

"I don't... want... to die..." I whispered between heavy breaths.

But more than that, I didn't want my *friends* to die. I wouldn't let them.

I had to follow in my father's footsteps in order to save

the earth. Whatever magic I had inside of me, it was strong enough to buy my friends more time.

It took all my willpower to blink away the tears and rise to my feet. I took one last glance at the portal. I didn't want to accept what was going to happen here, but I had to. Swallowing down the lump in my throat, I spread my wings and launched myself into the air.

I had to say goodbye before I made my sacrifice.

I landed on Marek's front lawn. The street was quiet, like everyone was in their own homes saying their goodbyes.

I approached the front door and raised my hand to knock, but before I could, the door swung open.

"Ryn!" Marek threw himself forward and pulled me into an embrace.

I laughed lightly, though it didn't feel like I should be laughing right now. "Did you miss me? I wasn't gone that long."

"I know," he said into my hair. "But I did miss you."

Marek let me go, and I stepped into the house.

I glanced around the empty living room. "Where is everyone?"

Marek raked his fingers through his untamed hair. "Allie and Kyle are with some people from school planning an end of the world party for tonight. I wanted to stay here so you knew where to find me."

"Where's your family?" I asked.

Marek dropped his gaze. "They've been gone for a couple of days. I told them to leave after the first attack on Eagle Valley. It was the best way to protect Bailey."

I inhaled a sharp breath. "And they just left you behind?"

Marek bit the inside of his cheek. "I didn't give them a choice."

Why did Marek always have to be so noble?

"I kind of regret it now," he said. "I'm not going to be able to say goodbye to them properly."

My heart broke for him.

"Marek." I stepped forward and placed my hands in his. "You don't have to be alone tonight. I'll stay with you." I rose to my toes and placed a kiss on the side of his face. "I promise."

A smile slowly touched his lips. "I'd like that."

Somehow, we ended up lying in Marek's bed, snacking on pretzels and fruit snacks.

I tossed an orange fruit snack toward the ceiling. Marek stretched away from me to catch it in his mouth. It bounced off his eyelid and onto my chest. I quickly snatched it up and popped it in my mouth with a smile. Marek frowned, like I was being unfair. I dug into my bag of fruit snacks for another, but they were all gone.

"Sorry," I told him as I tossed the wrapper on the floor.

Surprisingly, it was the first piece of trash I saw on his

carpet. I wasn't sure what I expected to find in Marek's room, but I didn't think it'd be so clean. Weren't guys supposed to be sloppy pigs?

I still couldn't get over the fact that I was in Marek's room. This was where he slept and did his homework. He probably spent his nights lying in this very bed staring up at this very ceiling thinking of me. Or so I liked to believe.

His navy blue comforter smelled like him. I wanted to take it home and put it on *my* bed. Then I remembered I'd never sleep in my own bed again, so it didn't matter.

"What's wrong?" Marek asked, noticing my sudden change of mood.

I snuggled into his chest and ran my fingers along the veins in his arms. My fingers trailed up to his chest before settling on my feather that hung around his neck. "Do you really have to ask that question?"

Marek sighed. "No. I guess not."

"I just wish we could've had more time together," I said honestly.

Marek pulled both arms around me and squeezed me tight. "I know. I wasted so much of the short time we had."

I drew away from him just enough to look into his eyes. "What do you mean?"

"I shouldn't have let Fletcher persuade me to leave you alone and treat you as only a training partner," he replied. "I should've told you how I felt right away. I shouldn't have been so caught up in my duty and been so scared."

My brows came together. "You were scared? Of me?"

Marek's eyes fixed on the ceiling. "I wasn't scared of

you. I was scared… to love you. I told you before, I have a hard time opening up to people."

I nodded. I remembered.

Marek took a long breath. "There's something you should know about me."

I immediately perked up.

Marek swallowed hard, but he didn't speak.

"What is it?" I prodded.

Marek fidgeted with the feather around my neck. "I'm sorry. It's just… hard. It's been so long since I talked about it."

I laced my fingers through his and waited for him to look at me. "You can tell me anything."

"I know," he whispered. "The thing is, my mother came from a Davina family, but she didn't develop Davina powers like her parents or sisters had. For all intents and purposes, she was entirely human."

I remained still, listening intently.

He paused for a beat. "She was resentful of her family and eventually cut herself off completely from them. That was before I was born. My dad was human, but he wasn't around much, so my mom was left to raise me by herself. She never mentioned her family, and I never asked."

Marek cleared his throat. "I always saw the Aedes, but my mom never acknowledged them. I told her about them once, but she made me swear I'd never mention them again. That should've been my first clue that something was out of the ordinary. Things didn't really change until I was ten."

"Change how?" I asked.

Marek continued slowly, like he wasn't sure how to tell the story. "We lived next to this big lake. There was one spot with a huge rock that stood about fifteen feet out of water. There was a rope swing tied to a tree above it. I never had any interest in jumping in. Honestly, I was afraid of heights as a kid. Seems ironic now, doesn't it?"

He didn't wait for an answer. "One day, I was walking alone on the rock. I slipped and fell, but I never touched the water. That was when I first discovered my wings."

I couldn't imagine what it was like for him to discover his wings on his own.

"I ran home and into the kitchen, thinking my mom would be able to help," Marek continued. "When she saw me, wings and all, she dropped the glass in her hand, and it shattered all over the floor. I tried to help her clean it up, but I cut my hand. It was so deep I thought we should go to the hospital, but she started yelling about how I wouldn't need stitches, that it was going to heal on its own because I was cursed. We started fighting. She mentioned the Davina, but obviously, I didn't know what she meant at the time."

Marek's tone softened. "To this day, I'm still not quite sure what we said to each other to make it escalate so far. But I remember how it ended."

His voice cracked, and I could already tell I wasn't going to like the rest of the story. "My mom reached out and grabbed one of my wings. With my wing in one hand and the piece of glass I cut myself on in the other, she sliced my wing clean off."

I inhaled an audible breath. I couldn't imagine what

kind of monster would do that to anyone, let alone their own son. It made me sick to my stomach to think about.

Tension grew in Marek's voice as he recounted the memory. "After she removed the second one, she stood and looked down at me. She didn't even seem to care that I was all bloody and crying. She said, *'There, James. I've fixed it. You're not a Davina anymore.'*"

It took everything I had to hold the tears back. I couldn't believe what Marek had been through.

"Marek, I'm *so* sorry," I whispered. I didn't know what else to say. There just weren't words for this kind of thing.

A muscle popped in his jaw. "She actually thought she was doing me a favor. Can you believe it?"

I couldn't bear it any longer. Silent tears began to fall down my cheeks as I stared, horrified, at the man beside me. For a moment, I thought I could spot the helpless ten-year-old inside of him.

Marek's eyes grew red. "That was only the first time she did it."

"Oh my god." I couldn't help but say *something*, even if I couldn't find the right words to tell him how sorry I was he had to go through that.

"Do you think I'd have these scars if it only happened once?" Marek asked, clearly not expecting an answer. "It wasn't long before the cut on my hand had healed and my wings started growing back. I wish I knew at that time that I could make them go away, but I didn't. Even if I could, I'm not sure now if I would've been able to hide them while they were healing. Anyway, I wasn't able to hide them from my mother. They weren't even healed completely before she cut them off again, yelling about how she couldn't believe she'd given birth to a Davina. I tried to get her to explain, but she never would."

"She sounds horrible," I said in a whisper.

Marek's expression hardened. "She was. It was three more years of hell with her. She wouldn't let me outside, and every time my wings grew back, she'd *take care of them for me.*"

"I can't even imagine."

"Good," Marek said in a clipped tone. "I don't want you to. No one should have to live through what I did."

He sighed again. "As I grew up and grew stronger, I eventually started fighting back. Then one day, I guess my mom gave up. She packed up the car with a bag of my stuff and drove me here, to Eagle Valley. She dropped me off at my aunt's house with a note, and that was the last I saw of her."

Marek balled his hands into fists. "The bitch didn't even have the courage to walk up to the front door and talk to her sister."

I couldn't believe this had really happened to him. It sounded like something you only saw in horror movies, not something that happened in real life. No wonder Marek talked so much about the evil in the world.

Marek's tone shifted. "I'm not scared to love you anymore, Ryn. You're the polar opposite of my mother. You're everything she wasn't. You're *good.*"

"I am?" I couldn't stop the words from spilling out of my mouth.

"Yes," Marek said. "I knew it when Dorian attacked you

in the woods. When I tried to kill him, you said there had to be an alternative. You said, *'You can't fight evil with evil.'*"

Did I really say that? I didn't remember.

Marek pushed a strand of hair from my eyes and spoke softly. "I knew there was something special about you because no one had ever thought of it like that with the demons. No one ever tried to make peace with them like you have. This whole time, you've been trying to see the good in them."

I blinked back tears. I hadn't realized how much of an impact I had on Marek.

"I wish I would've loved you fully when I had the chance," Marek said.

I pushed myself up to sit. "What do you mean, Marek? We still have time."

He shook his head. "I'll never be able to take you on a nice date or to a dance or anything."

I rose to my feet and pulled at his arm. "This isn't a date?"

Marek followed my lead and stood. I wrapped my arms around his neck, and his hands settled on my waist.

I swayed my body. "We can dance right here."

Marek closed his eyes and rested his forehead on mine. He shifted his weight from one foot to the other. "There isn't any music."

"We don't need music to dance," I whispered.

Marek didn't seem to agree with me. He began humming the soft, slow tune to one of my favorite songs while we swayed in a circle.

"How'd you know I loved that song?" I asked.

Marek shrugged. "I didn't."

His melodic voice filled my ears and warmed my heart. How had it taken me this long to learn Marek had an amazing voice?

His humming turned into lyrics.

We don't have to talk.
The tears don't have to fall.
Lie down next to me;
We'll forget about it all.

I melted into him, pressing my body against his while he sang to me. A wave of conflicting emotions consumed me. I was beyond happy to be here in his arms but devastated that it wasn't going to last. It wasn't fair that we didn't have more time. It wasn't fair that we weren't going to grow old together.

All we had was tonight. And my body burned to make these last few hours we had count.

My lips crashed into his, silencing the music coming from them. Marek tensed in surprise but quickly relaxed.

I gasped when he swept my feet out from under me and tossed me onto the bed. My body trembled as Marek climbed on top of me. My hands locked on the side of his face, and I guided his lips up to meet mine again.

Marek kissed me gently. Too gently.

I wanted more. I wanted him. Every last bit he'd share with me.

I ran my hands across his back. My fingers momentarily crossed the scars along his shoulder blades, and I was instantly reminded of the story he'd just told me. Now, more than ever, I wanted to share myself with him, to heal his emotional scars, to make everything better.

I knew I could never do that, but the least I could do was try. Because I loved him.

The thought struck me hard. Did I *love* Marek?

Yes, I told myself instantly.

There was no question about it. I loved this man with all my heart, and I'd be damned if I didn't show him just how much he meant to me.

I drew away from him.

Marek propped himself up and looked down at me. "What?"

I stared into his eyes, burning the beautiful blue color into my mind. By now, I'd memorized the pattern of brown flecks in his irises.

"I just wanted you to know I love you, Marek," I whispered.

A wide smile brightened his face. "I love you, too, Ryn."

I knew with every fiber of my being that he meant it. I flung my arms around him again and pulled him back onto me. Our bodies collided like magnets.

Marek's hands found the thin line of exposed skin between my tank top and jeans. He slowly inched his fingers up my body, exposing more and more skin.

Finally, they reached the fabric of my bra. Marek pulled away.

I bit my lower lip and stretched my arms above my head.

Marek hesitated. "I—I've never—"

"Me, either," I told him.

"Are you sure?" he asked gently.

"I'm sure," I whispered breathlessly.

My heart hammered against the inside of my chest as the cool air touched my skin. If at any moment I thought my heart might stop out of fear or excitement, it was nothing compared to this.

I was going to die of a heart attack for sure.

It didn't matter how I died, as long as I got to spend this night with Marek.

Somehow, tonight felt like my first—and my last—night on earth.

Marek stirred next to me, waking me. I blinked my eyes open to see the morning sun filling the room and illuminating his gorgeous body beside me. Happiness filled my chest, but it quickly disappeared when reality hit me.

My time with Marek was already over.

The smile that had started creeping across my face faded before it had a chance to fully form. Tears welled in my eyes.

Marek suddenly became alert. "Ryn, what's wrong?"

"Nothing," I lied.

I sniffled involuntarily. Dammit. Now was *not* the time to let him see me cry.

"I'm just not ready to go home yet." I reluctantly peeled myself away from him and sat up in the bed. The comforter we'd been cuddling under covered my chest.

Marek touched my shoulder. "You don't have to go."

I reached for my clothes on the ground and began

pulling them on. I didn't look at him; I couldn't bear to right now.

"I do have to go," I insisted. "I have to say goodbye to my mom."

I stood and reached down to slip my shoes on. Marek sat up straight. His exposed chest distracted me momentarily, but I forced my gaze back up to his eyes.

"Is that *all* you're going to do?" he asked.

"Mm-hmm," I lied again. How did he know me so well?

"You're sure?" he pressed.

I took a deep breath and forced the tears away. After last night, it didn't seem fair to lie to him. But I knew if I told him the truth, he'd only try to stop me.

"Yes." My chest compressed. I was a bad liar.

Marek frowned. He didn't believe me.

He pushed back the covers and reached for his jeans. "I'll come with you."

"No," I said, almost too quickly. "I'll be fine. I want to talk to my mom alone."

"Okay." It still didn't sound like he was buying it.

I bent over the bed to place one last kiss on his lips. I swallowed down the lump in my throat. It took everything I had to keep the tears from spilling over the edge. I didn't want to leave him.

My fingers remained on the side of his face a moment too long. I wanted to tell him I'd see him later, but that was one lie I couldn't bring myself to spit out.

Instead, I told him the truth. "I love you."

Before I left the room, the last words I'd ever hear Marek speak reached my ears.

"I love you, too."

I raked my fingers through my hair on the walk to my house. Maybe Mom would believe I was out flying all night and not getting tangled in Hot Stuff's sheets.

I laughed internally. She could probably sense the teenage hormones from here.

The old wooden porch steps creaked under my weight. I opened the front door and quietly stepped into the house.

Mom stood in the hallway with a hand on her hip and her lips pursed. She'd been waiting for me.

"Mom, please," I said. "Can we not fight right now?"

"Are you going to be honest with me?" She tapped her foot. She actually *tapped her foot*.

"Depends…" There were things I couldn't tell her.

"Where were you last night?" she demanded.

Okay, that one I *could* tell her. I just didn't *want* to.

"Don't play the silent game with me," she warned. "I already know where you were."

What the hell? How did she know?

"Then why are you asking?" I replied.

Ugh. Did we really need to do this *again*? All I wanted was to snuggle up next to my mom like I did when I was five. Now that I was facing her, I wasn't sure that would help anything.

"I was hoping you'd be honest with me," she said. "I know you went to that party with Allie last night."

Oh. Well, she could think that all she wanted. I wasn't going to correct her.

"Who told you that?" I asked, partially out of my own curiosity.

Mom crossed her arms. "When you didn't come home last night, I went over to Allie's to see if you were there. Her dad said you two were at some party. I just can't believe you never called or anything."

"My phone is broken," I reminded her.

"I know," she said, "but you could've used Allie's phone to call. I just wanted to hear your voice. I wanted to know you were all right and not lying in the ditch somewhere after being thrown off the back of your boyfriend's motorcycle."

I was so shocked that I actually took a step back. Mom wasn't *mad* at me. She was *worried.* And unfortunately for both of us, her worry manifested in anger. Why hadn't I realized that until now?

A silent beat passed between us. I couldn't take it any longer. I stepped toward her and flung my arms around her neck.

Mom's body tensed in surprise. "Kathryn, what's wrong?"

I shook my head. The truth was too overwhelming. "I'm just sorry. I never meant to make you worry."

Mom rubbed my back. "You're my daughter. I worry about you all the time."

"I'm okay, Mom. I promise." I drew away from her. "Did you have breakfast yet?"

She shook her head.

"What do you say we make some pancakes?" I suggested.

Mom brushed her fingers under her eyes. "I'd like that."

Life had been so hectic lately that I hadn't had many chances to cook. It was nice to be back in the kitchen again. I spent extra time getting the pancake recipe just right. I knew it would be the last meal I ever ate.

Mom pulled orange juice from the fridge and set the table while I cooked. Silence settled over the kitchen, but for the first time in a long time, there wasn't tension in the air between us.

"Hey, Mom," I said as I flipped a pancake.

She sat in one of the kitchen chairs. "Yeah?"

"I was just wondering… Which phase was your favorite?"

"Phase?" she asked with raised eyebrows.

"Yeah." I shrugged. "You know how you go through phases. Which one did you like best?"

"What do you mean, phases?" She looked completely baffled.

Oh my god. Mom didn't know she went through phases. Something about jumping from one hobby to the next must've seemed so natural to her. Maybe that was why she never encouraged me to choose something and stick with it.

"You really don't know?" I asked.

Mom shook her head.

"You're always changing hobbies," I pointed out. "You work through them almost as fast as we move. I thought you realized."

"Ooh," Mom said in realization. "I just like to try new things, Kathryn. There's nothing wrong with that."

I poured more pancake batter into the pan. "I never said there was anything wrong with it. I just wanted to know what you liked best."

Mom shrugged. "Well, I like all of my hobbies."

"Including sewing?" I tried to hide my teasing smile.

Mom rolled her eyes. "Okay, maybe not sewing. What were my other phases?"

I didn't even have to think about it to begin listing them. "Martial arts. Running. Photography. Scrapbooking. Cooking—"

"Cooking," Mom cut me off.

"Cooking?"

"Yeah, that one was my favorite."

Huh. Mine, too.

"Why?" I asked.

Mom stood and reached out for the spatula in my hand. "Because that's the one I had the most fun doing with you."

She flipped the pancake and smiled at me. I couldn't help but smile back.

It felt eerie sitting across from my mom and watching her eat without her knowing this was the last time she would ever see me.

After we finished and I helped her wash the dishes, Mom took a look at the clock on the stove. "What are your plans for the day?"

I hesitated. I had no choice but to lie to her. "I have some training scheduled for today."

My feet remained grounded in the kitchen. I wasn't

ready to go. I didn't know what Mom would do without me. But I had to do it—for everyone else.

I pulled Mom into a hug. This time, she didn't seem surprised by it.

"I love you, Mom."

"I love you, too, Kathryn."

We embraced longer than any sane mother and daughter would've. I didn't care if it meant Mom could tell something was up. I just wanted to keep her in my arms and inhale the scent of her strawberry shampoo for hours. I wished I could make up for all the nights we fought instead of snuggled up in front of the TV like we should've.

I squeezed her tighter. "Mom, I want you to know that I admire you for how strong you are."

She opened her mouth to speak, but I didn't let her.

"Whatever happens with this Davina stuff, I want you to keep fighting no matter what," I said. "You always have to keep fighting."

"I wish you didn't have to do this," Mom whispered.

For a moment, I thought she might know what I was planning, but then I realized she meant she wished I didn't have to fight with the Davina. She didn't want to lose me like she had my father.

"I'm sorry."

Those two simple words held so much more meaning than she could possibly know.

～

Nerves hit my stomach when I stepped out of the house. Cool air touched my skin, and a thin layer of clouds covered the sky. It was starting to feel and smell like autumn.

It was almost time.

Almost.

There was still one more person I had to see.

I crossed my lawn and headed up Allie's front porch steps. I held my breath and knocked on the door. I wasn't sure if I was ready to see Allie for the last time. Saying goodbye to her would be harder than saying goodbye to my mom—or even Marek.

No answer came, and I wasn't sure if I was upset or relieved. I was just about to knock again when the sound of voices reached my ears.

Allie and Kyle.

I followed the sound of their voices around the side of the house and stopped when I finally saw them. They swayed in the swings on Allie's old playset with their backs to me. They moved back and forth in sync with their fingers entwined.

I had the sudden urge to step back around the corner of the house unseen. I couldn't ruin their moment. I pressed my body against the vinyl siding.

"I'm not ready for this, Kyle." Allie's voice traveled through the light breeze toward me. "I've dreamt of becoming a Protector my whole life. I never imagined I wouldn't make it that far."

"I know," Kyle's deep voice replied.

"There are other things, too," Allie said in disappointment. "I always thought I'd have kids and that we'd—"

Her words stopped in their tracks.

"We'd what?" Kyle asked.

Allie tucked her dark hair behind her ear. "I can't believe I'm saying this, but I always thought that one day we'd get together and… I always pictured us growing old together."

Kyle dug his heels into the dirt and stopped swaying. I expected him to say something to her, but instead, he reached out for her and caught her mid-swing. She gasped in surprise, but before she had a chance to say anything, Kyle's lips were on hers.

I resisted the urge to start cheering from where I hid. *Finally* they'd gotten together! I was so happy for Allie that it was almost as if her own happiness filled my heart.

I forced my gaze off the happy couple and returned around the side of the house. It wasn't fair of me to watch their happy moment unfold without their consent.

"Allie," I whispered under my breath. She'd never hear my words, but for a moment, it felt as if the wind could carry them over to her for me. "I can't believe we've only been friends for a few months. It feels like a lifetime."

I took a deep breath. It felt silly to talk out loud to myself, but I needed to say these words, even if she'd never receive the message. "I wish we'd met sooner and had more time together. I wish Marek and I could've grown old alongside you and Kyle. I wish… I wish for a lot of things, but honestly, I'm just glad I got the time with you that I did. You're my best friend, Allie. And I hope that what I'm about to do gives you the chance to live your dreams—for a few more years, anyway."

I swallowed down the lump in my throat. "I love you, Allie."

I couldn't bear to look back. If I did, I might not be able to bring myself to leave.

And so, I flexed my shoulders and leapt into the air.

I was finally ready to make my sacrifice.

The town was quiet today as I flew above it. It was like Eagle Valley itself had given up hope with the rest of the Davina.

Someone see me. Stop me, I begged internally.

No one did.

An audible breath passed my lips when I landed in the clearing and looked up at the portal. The ripples in the air had grown so large that they looked like waves. The trees behind the portal were so distorted that it was impossible to make them out.

As I stepped forward, a strange breeze passed across my arms. It was warmer than the air around me, but something about it chilled me to the bone. The hairs on my arms stood, and a burnt scent hung in the air. It wasn't the pleasant scent of a burning fire during winter. It was more like the smell of a hot car or burnt rubber—the scent that told you to stop whatever the hell you were doing before something exploded.

Could that strange air be coming from the portal? From Malum?

I stopped two yards from the portal and steadied myself. My head swirled as I stared into the distorted air. I closed my eyes so it wouldn't distract me and called upon my white wispy essence. I felt it rise from my toes and up into my shoulders. It flowed smoothly down my arms, reaching my elbows, then my wrists.

Before it reached my fingertips, something hard slammed into my side. The air left my lungs as I crashed to the ground. I didn't have time to catch myself. I landed on my shoulder before the side of my head smacked into the ground.

I opened my eyes to try to make sense of what had just happened, but the sky swam above me. Had I been sucked into the portal?

No. Some asshole had tackled me.

Anthony Lucas's face came into view above me.

Yep. Some asshole.

"What the—?" I started to say.

Before I could get the words out, Anthony's shiny black shoe connected with my face.

Everything went black.

Deep voices met my ears, but I couldn't focus long enough to make out what they were saying. My head lolled to the side.

Where was I? Was I moving? It felt like my body was bouncing. Over potholes?

No. I was being carried. And we were descending a flight of steps.

I gathered what strength I had and peeled my eyes open. Wherever I was, it was dark. I could just barely make out Anthony's face above me. We reached the bottom of the steps, and I felt Anthony drop me onto a cold, hard surface. His footsteps retreated and then stopped.

The sound of a door swinging shut was like an alarm to my ears. Suddenly, I was alert. I shot up to a sitting position. Bad idea. My head pounded like a bass drum.

I blinked several times, and my eyes finally adjusted to the darkness. I looked up to see a flight of wooden stairs above me. They rose to meet a dark wood door. A click sounded.

I scrambled to my feet and scurried up the stairs. "Hey!" I shouted as I wrenched on the door handle. "You can't just leave me here!"

I pounded my fists against the door, but no answer came. My heart dropped from my chest, down the stairs, and straight onto the concrete floor below me. At least, it felt like it.

I screamed in frustration as I twisted on the door knob and kicked the door. My foot throbbed now, and the screaming didn't help my headache.

I stopped abruptly and quieted, though my chest continued to heave as I inhaled deep breaths. My eyes scanned the stairwell I stood in. It looked familiar. I descended several steps and looked out into the vast room they'd locked me in. A low ceiling was held up by support pillars, and small windows lining the top of the walls allowed a slight amount of light to filter in. Across the room, I spotted the old foam targets we used for training in the corner.

I was in the basement of Galen High School.

And somehow, the Davina Council had found time to switch the door knob so it locked from the outside.

There must be a way out. I had to find it and get back to the portal before it destroyed us all.

I went with my first instinct. I turned back to the door and conjured a white fireball, aiming it toward the new door knob. The fireball smashed into the door and exploded like a firecracker. When I stepped forward to see if it'd done any damage, the door looked perfectly fine. I cursed under my breath.

"It's no use," a voice said.

I jumped back and almost tripped down the stairs. I caught myself and peered across the dark room.

"I thought I was alone," I said, like that would explain my madness. "Who's there?"

A feminine voice cleared her throat. The last person I expected to see stepped out of the shadows and into the dim light.

"Casey?" I asked in surprise.

Of course it's Casey, you dimwit.

She stood just feet away from me. I could make out her features clear as day. Bags had settled beneath her eyes, and her lips were chapped. Her face was bare of makeup.

"How long have you been down here?" I asked. "You look like hell."

Casey sighed and sank onto one of the lower steps. "I've been down here since last night."

"Why would they—?"

"I followed my dad and tried eavesdropping on their council meeting." Casey stared forward into the darkness without looking at me. "Grace wanted the council to surround the portal and keep an eye on it."

In other words, Grace didn't want me trying anything. After yesterday's catastrophe, she still believed the world needed to end.

"So Grace changed her mind again," I said under my breath as I lowered myself beside Casey.

"I was going to go find you and tell you before they had a chance to get out there. I thought maybe you had an idea to save us." Casey eyed me curiously. "You do have an idea, don't you?"

I bit my lip. "I have something worth trying. What happened after you overheard the council?"

Casey's expression hardened. "Anthony was there—like, right behind me—watching me eavesdrop. He grabbed me by the hair and dragged me down here."

I gasped. *That dick!*

"He said he couldn't let me out with all the stuff I heard."

I crossed my arms—and not just because it was chilly down here. "So, Grace has them all wrapped around her little finger?"

Obviously.

Casey pursed her lips and nodded. "I've spent all night trying to get out of here to warn you they'd be there. I figured you'd try to go back, but nothing I've done has worked."

"Lovely," I said flatly. "What are we supposed to do? Just sit around and wait for the realms to collapse?"

Casey dropped her gaze. "What other choice do we have? Unless you have your phone on you to call for help. They took mine."

I shook my head and got to my feet. "No, I don't, but we can't just give up."

Casey chewed on her thumb nail. "What are we supposed to do?"

"I don't know," I sighed.

The sound of a key in the door reached my ears. My head snapped in the direction of the door.

"Maybe we can seduce this one to let us out," I whispered under my breath.

Casey's eyes fell on the man who opened the door. "Uh, sorry, but that's not going to work on him."

Mr. Harris took one look at Casey and rushed down the steps. Casey got to her feet just as he reached her. He wrapped her in a hug. A moment later, the door slammed shut, making me jump. I heard the audible click of the lock slipping back into place.

"Dad!" Casey cried. "What are you doing here? I thought the Davina Council wouldn't trust you—"

"They don't," he interrupted.

I stood there awkwardly, watching this family reunion I wasn't a part of.

Mr. Harris drew away from Casey. "I convinced them to let me visit you. I wanted to stay with you until the end."

Casey shook her head. "No, Dad. You can't give up! You have to get us out of here."

Mr. Harris looked hopeless. "I—I can't."

"Can't? Or won't? You still agree with Grace, don't you?" Casey stepped away from him, as if she'd been betrayed.

Mr. Harris rubbed his eyes, like this had all become too much for him. "Grace has watched the history of the world. She knows things the rest of us don't."

"And you're just blindly following her!" Casey yelled, taking another step away from him.

Mr. Harris frowned. "I don't understand why you don't have any faith in her. I thought I raised you differently."

I inched away into the shadows. This didn't seem like the kind of family fight I should be involved in.

"You *raised* me to think logically," Casey bit back. "I can think for myself, and I don't think Grace's plan is a good one."

"Our essence will survive," Mr. Harris pointed out, but it sounded more like he was trying to convince himself of that.

Casey shook her head. "You don't know that. Our essence lives inside the earth. If it's destroyed—"

"I know." Her dad cut her off. He dropped his shoulders and took a long breath before speaking again. "I know. Some of the councilmembers have their doubts. But Casey, there's nothing we can do."

"Then what is Grace protecting the portal from?" Casey asked.

"I—" Mr. Harris stopped mid-breath, like he hadn't considered the question until now.

"Ryn has a plan." Casey's eyes traveled over to me.

Mr. Harris's gaze followed.

I shifted my weight uncomfortably between my feet.

Mr. Harris sighed. "Even if I wanted to let you go, they locked me down here with you."

"Then at least help us find a way to escape," Casey begged.

Mr. Harris's jaw tensed. "There *is* one thing we can try."

Casey and her dad exchanged a look, as if they shared some telepathic conversation I wasn't a part of.

"What?" I asked. "How are we going to escape?"

"Just watch." Casey smirked. "And be ready to run." She turned back to her dad and erupted in anger. "What are you doing here? I don't want to see you!"

I recoiled in shock.

"I came because I love you." Mr. Harris's voice rose.

Oh. They were putting on a show.

Casey screamed again. "It's too late for that! You let them throw me down here. I was hungry and thirsty and scared!"

Okay, maybe it wasn't *all* for show.

Mr. Harris huffed and turned back up the stairs. His fists pounded on the door. "Let me out, Harold! I've changed my mind. My daughter is being a *brat*, and I have better ways to spend my time."

"No can do," came a voice on the other side of the door.

"What are you talking about?" Mr. Harris demanded. "I told you to let me out!"

"Boss said I'm not to open this door for anyone," Harold replied, sounding uncertain.

"Surely Grace didn't mean me," Mr. Harris snarled. "I came down here voluntarily."

Harold didn't answer.

"Harold!" Mr. Harris shouted with a tone of authority. "The world is ending, and I have better people to say goodbye to than an ungrateful teenager."

I leaned over and whispered to Casey. "Does he really think you're ungrateful?"

She shrugged. "Probably, but if he saves our lives, he can apologize later." She raised her voice and projected it up the stairwell. "Seriously, Harold. Let my dad go. I'd rather die down here alone!" She threw in a couple of heavy sobs for show.

Damn. What was this girl doing training to become a Protector? She should've been training to become an actress.

"Where are the girls?" Harold called through the door.

"At the bottom of the stairs," Mr. Harris answered. "Why?"

"Everyone step back," Harold instructed. "I want the girls as far away from the door as possible."

Mr. Harris winked over his shoulder. "Okay," he answered. "You can open the door now."

My knees shook in anticipation. I heard the lock on the other side of the door click. Slowly, the door handle twisted.

Mr. Harris sprung straight into action. He rammed his shoulder into the door, knocking the guy on the other side of it down. Mr. Harris shot two fireballs straight into Harold's chest. Harold crumbled to the ground.

Ouch.

"Come on," Mr. Harris hissed, gesturing for us to follow him.

Casey and I rushed up the stairs side-by-side. Her dad placed his index finger over his lips and stepped over Harold's still body. We followed behind him, careful not to make too much noise.

"This way," he whispered, leading us to the back of the building. His eyes darted around the hall.

My heart slammed against my rib cage. *They're going to catch us. There's no time. We're not going to make it out of here alive.*

Mr. Harris carefully looked around the corner before gesturing that it was safe. The sound I'd been dreading reached my ears when we turned down the hall. A door creaked open, and then—

"Hey!" someone shouted. "What are you—?"

My heart leapt in my chest.

Mr. Harris turned around, almost ramming into us. "Go! I'll hold them off."

Casey's feet moved under her, but she hesitated. "But, Dad—"

"No arguing!" he roared. "Run!"

Two... Three... Five... I couldn't keep track of how many pairs of footsteps followed behind us. Shouts echoed down the hall as more Davina Council members joined in on the chase.

What are they all doing here? I thought. *They should be saying goodbye to their loved ones, not hanging out at the school.*

Maybe they didn't have loved ones. That, or their duty to Grace came first. I wasn't interested in sticking around to find out which it was.

I heard the familiar sound of essence exploding against the ground, but I didn't look back to see what was going on. Casey and I turned down another hall, and I instantly felt my body being jerked to the side.

"In here," Casey hissed as she dragged me along behind her.

Casey and I raced through the library, the dark mahogany bookcases blurring together as we sped by. She led me down a narrow hallway and through another door. She quickly swung it shut behind us and secured the lock.

I glanced around while trying to catch my breath. White overwhelmed my senses—white walls, white tile, a white toilet, and a white sink. There was even a white radiator in the corner of the small bathroom.

Casey cursed under her breath. "We shouldn't have left my dad out there. The Davina Council is going to kill him."

I caught Casey before she could reach the door. "You don't know that. They'll probably just lock him up again."

Casey struggled out of my grasp.

"Stop it!" I whisper-screamed. "We have no chance of saving him if we get caught, too."

Casey relaxed slightly. "Then we have to get out of here before they find us."

She quickly crossed the bathroom and reached for the lock on the window. She grunted as she tried to push it open. I hurried over to help her. We pushed up on the window together, but even with all our strength, it didn't slide open.

"The damn thing's been painted shut." Casey turned away from it and sank down onto the closed toilet lid. I noticed her knees were visibly shaking. "We'll wait it out for a couple of minutes. Just to make sure."

I raised my eyebrows. "And if they find us?"

"We'll break the window." She paused for a moment. "So, what's your plan?"

It felt awkward to open up to Casey, but I knew she was on my side. Still, I struggled to swallow my pride and admit it.

I leaned against the window sill. "I discovered this… strange essence. I don't know if I'm the only one who has it, but it seems powerful enough to affect the portal. I already tried it, and it did something, but it wasn't enough."

Casey raised her eyebrows like she didn't believe me. "A new kind of essence?"

I nodded and held my hand out. I narrowed my eyes at my palm, concentrating hard. It was like the first time I discovered essence and couldn't conjure a basic fireball to save my life. I knew I had it in me, but I couldn't seem to access it at will. I concentrated harder and harder, until I thought my head might explode from the tension. Casey must've thought for sure I was talking shit. The tingling sensation in my body grew, until finally, white smoke escaped my fingertips and swirled into an orb above my palm.

Casey straightened and eyed the essence in wonder. Slowly, she reached out with her index finger, but before she touched it, she jerked away like she'd been shocked.

"Have you ever seen anything like it?" I asked.

She shook her head, never taking her eyes off the orb. "What is it?"

I shrugged and let the essence dissipate. Holding it there for that long was draining. "I don't know. I could only do it after I woke Grace."

Casey never took her eyes off my hand, even though the essence wasn't there anymore. "You're sure it's essence?"

I furrowed my brow. "What else would it be? It feels like essence. Just… different."

"What do you mean, different?"

I didn't have a chance to answer. I fell silent the moment male voices met my ears.

"You go that way," one of them called to the other.

Casey and I both held our breath as footsteps passed by the door we hid behind. We breathed a collective sigh of relief when the footsteps continued down the hall.

Casey turned her eyes back to me. "What are you going to do with this new essence?"

I bit my lower lip. I didn't know how it'd sound to admit the rest out loud. Probably crazy. Maybe I was crazy.

I took a breath. "I thought if I entered the portal and used the essence inside it, it might collapse—even partially—and buy everyone a little more time."

"No." Casey shook her head in protest.

"What do you mean, no?" The surface of my skin heated involuntarily. I had the urge to throw another fireball at Casey's face when she blatantly dismissed my plan, but I had to remind myself that we were on the same side. It was still weird to me.

"You're talking about *killing* yourself!" Casey hissed.

Her words should've tore at my heart. I should've felt sick to my stomach and begged her to talk me out of it. Instead, I felt a strange sense of peace wash over me.

"Yes, I am," I answered.

"You can't!" she objected under her breath.

I raised an eyebrow. "Do you have a better plan?"

Her shoulders fell. "No. But even if your plan worked, you can't exactly go sacrificing yourself when the Davina Council is watching the portal."

"Maybe you can distract them," I suggested.

She looked at me with an unamused expression. "How?"

"I don't know." I shrugged. "Strip naked and run around the clearing."

Casey rolled her eyes.

"It's the end of the world," I pointed out. "There's no time to be modest."

"You just want to watch me make a fool out of myself," she said lightheartedly.

I smirked. "Maybe."

Casey turned serious again. "Let's just take a breath, and we'll figure something else out."

I shook my head. "We don't have time."

"We don't know how much time we have," Casey pointed out. "It could be days or—"

"—or hours," I finished for her. "Let's get out of here, and then we'll figure out how to distract the Davina Council."

Casey frowned. "You're going to do this with or without my help, aren't you?"

I nodded.

Casey hesitated but eventually rose to her feet. Slowly, she unlocked the door and peered out into the hall.

"It's clear," she whispered.

We slipped out of the library unnoticed, but my footsteps sounded like cannons going off. I was sure I'd alert the Davina Council. The back door of the school stood at the end of the hall. We were so close, but it felt like a mile away.

Almost there.

Someone was going to jump out and get us. I knew it.

Except, by some miracle, we reached the end of the hall and broke out into the cool autumn air without being spotted.

"Ryn!" a voice shouted my name.

Shit. I spoke too soon.

Wait… no. I knew that voice. I stopped, and Casey skidded to a halt beside me.

Marek jogged down the steps behind the school to catch up with us. Allie and Kyle followed behind him.

"Marek, I—" I started.

"Where have you been?" Concern was etched into his tone. He reached for my hands and inspected my arms and then my face, searching for signs of injury. "You said you'd be back. We've been searching everywhere for you."

I inhaled a heavy breath. "Marek, I'm sorry. I—"

"We don't have time for this," Casey said in a rush.

I followed her gaze to see two Davina Council members in one of the windows pointing across the lawn at us. They quickly turned away from the window and rushed out of the room.

"They're coming!" Casey cried.

Marek glanced over his shoulder.

"Who?" Allie demanded. "What's going on?"

I didn't have time to explain. "We need to get out of here—now."

Casey spread her wings beside me, and I quickly followed. I heard Marek's, Allie's, and Kyle's wings flapping behind me. I pumped my wings harder and pushed ahead of Casey. I wasn't sure where I was going until I spotted a rocky hilltop and dove for it.

I landed on the granite without stumbling. *Finally* someone saw me land like a proper Davina.

I paced along the top of the hill. I wasn't sure why I brought everyone here. This was *mine and Marek's* hilltop. Marek landed next to me, and without thinking, I fell into his arms.

Marek squeezed me but drew away far too soon. "Ryn, what's happening?"

"I wanted to—I tried to—the Davina Council—" I couldn't manage to choke out the words.

"Take a deep breath," Kyle suggested. He looked genuinely concerned for me.

"Maybe you should sit down," Allie said.

I gladly complied with her invitation and sank to the ground. Marek knelt beside me.

Casey placed her hands on her hips and tried to catch her breath. "The Davina Council locked Ryn and me in the basement. They don't want anyone trying anything with the portal."

Marek's head snapped in Casey's direction. "What were you trying to do with the portal?"

Casey huffed. "It wasn't me. It was Ryn."

"Casey, don't—" I started, but the words were already flying out of her mouth.

"She's going to sacrifice herself to buy us time."

"No!" Marek objected at the same time Allie's hands shot over her mouth. Kyle stared at me speechlessly from beside her.

"Casey's lying," Marek accused.

She frowned. "I wish I was."

"You can't!" Marek roared. He shot to his feet and paced in front of me. He raked his hands through his hair, and his face contorted in pain.

"Marek, I—" I started.

"You were just going to leave me?" he shouted, cutting me off. "You lied to me!"

"I had to!" I cried. "I knew you'd try to stop me. Marek, if I don't do this, everyone will die. The least I can do is give the rest of you a chance."

"If you do this, *you'll* die!" Marek growled.

I dropped my gaze. My voice came out as only a whisper. "I know that, and..."

Marek stopped pacing and lowered himself to sit beside me on the ground. His fingers grazed the side of my face, and I was forced to look at him. His tone softened. "If you're going to die, we're going to die together."

He doesn't mean that, I told myself.

I spoke softly. "You're the one who said you wouldn't let my father's death be in vain. This is the only way."

"But it won't work," Allie protested.

I looked up to see a deeply hurt expression settled on her face.

"You don't have the Power of Grace anymore," Allie pointed out. "Your essence isn't strong enough."

"I have something else, though," I said. "Remember?"

Kyle glanced to Allie in uncertainty. "You said you felt something when Malcolm kidnapped you, but Ryn, you couldn't even control it when you tried to show us."

"It's still inside of me," I argued.

"It doesn't matter!" Allie burst. "You can't sacrifice yourself!"

"Why not?" I asked. "My dad bought us eighteen years. I can buy the rest of you a few more. Maybe it'll give you enough time to figure out a permanent solution."

"We can't lose you!" Allie declared.

Marek's eyes glistened with tears. "Allie's right. We can't lose you." He took my hand in his and brought it to his lips. "*I* can't lose you."

Didn't they realize they'd lose me either way?

"See?" Casey said. "I'm not the only one who thinks you shouldn't sacrifice yourself."

"Maybe there's something else we can do," Allie suggested.

"Like what?" Casey asked.

Allie looked uncertain. "What if we turned to Malcolm?"

Kyle eyed Allie like she was crazy. "What's that going to accomplish?"

Allie bit her lower lip. "Maybe the Aedes have some insight. Maybe they can help."

I could hardly believe she was the one suggesting it. All this time, Allie had been lecturing me about how evil the Aedes were. Now she wanted to side with them?

I thought about how Malcolm had mentioned that the Davina never listened to the Aedes. Maybe they had stories—knowledge—about their history they never shared. Maybe they *did* have something we could use against the portal, against Grace.

I straightened. "I think we should do it. At the very least, he and the other Aedes might be able to help us reach the portal before it's too late."

The air felt eerie and cold when we arrived at Malcolm's house. I knew we'd established a truce, but I still approached the house with caution.

"Malcolm?" I called out, peering into the slit between the curtains.

No response.

"Malcolm?" I raised my voice and entered the house. "Are you here?"

I peeked into the dark living room while Marek checked the kitchen. Kyle headed to the end of the hall and poked his head into a bedroom, and Allie followed Casey upstairs. They returned a minute later, and we all exchanged a look of disappointment.

My shoulders dropped. We didn't have time for this. "He said this is where I could find him if I needed to."

"Maybe he was lying," Kyle theorized.

"He wasn't," I said with certainty.

"Well, he is a de—" Kyle started.

"An Aedes?" The sound of Malcolm's voice cut Kyle off before he could finish the insult.

I whirled around to see Malcolm standing in the front doorway with his hood down.

The look Malcolm gave Kyle could've cut glass. "I thought we had a truce."

"We do," I assured him. "And we need your help."

I quickly explained to Malcolm what was going on. His expression softened the more I revealed.

"Can you help us?" I asked hopefully.

Malcolm pressed his lips into a thin line. "There might be something I can do, but it's a long shot."

Without another word, Malcolm turned from the doorway. Then he spread his dark, feathery wings and gestured for us to follow him.

25

We landed on the gravel outside of an old building at the edge of the small town Malcolm lived near. Trees surrounded the property, but I noticed a cluster of run-down houses up the road.

The building in front of us was at least six times bigger than my house, and most of the white paint had chipped away. The concrete walkway leading to the front doors heaved at odd angles and had thick grass growing up between each slab. The sidewalk twisted around the side of the building and ended at a small cemetery. I lifted my gaze to view the bell tower above us.

I noted how strange it was that demons were taking refuge in an old church. Except, they weren't demons any more than we were angels.

I took a cautious step forward. Malcolm approached the church like he was completely comfortable here, but the twisted trees above my head and the cemetery just a stone's throw away gave me the creeps.

"Come on," Malcolm hissed.

I quickened my paced and followed behind him. He didn't stop at the front doors like I expected him to. Instead, he headed around the side of the church.

"We settled here after the last attack," Malcolm explained. "We needed somewhere the Davina couldn't see us from the sky, and this seemed like the least likely place you'd look for us. It's been abandoned for decades. There's a broken window in the back you can get through."

Tall windows lined the side of the building. Most had been covered by wood from the inside. Malcolm stopped at the one on the end and gestured for us to follow. He phased straight through the wall as if he were a ghost. The window had been broken in the lower right-hand corner, but the opening was hardly enough to crawl through.

Marek apparently thought the same thing. "Stand back," he warned.

I jumped aside just in time for him to swing a fistful of rock at the remaining half of the window, shattering it.

We all stared at him in shock.

Marek shrugged. "It was already broken." He turned back to the window and hoisted himself up and through it. I followed behind him.

"Careful," Marek's voice came through the darkness.

I stepped onto a wooden floor in a large room with a high vaulted ceiling. I expected to find rows of pews lined up throughout the chapel, but they'd all been removed. Glass crunched under my feet, and a pile of beer bottles and cigarette butts lay just a few feet away.

Then there were the eyes. Hundreds of pairs of Aedes

eyes stared back at us. They all had their hoods down, like they always wore them like this in private. Despite their thin, pale features, I felt like I was looking into the faces of humans—not the evil creatures the Davina made them out to be.

Silence fell over the church. The only sound I heard was the brush of Kyle's jeans against the window frame as he crawled into the chapel.

"*Davina*," one of the closest Aedes hissed through clenched teeth.

As soon as he said it, three of the Aedes lunged for Marek and me. I instinctively yelped and jumped backward.

Malcolm raised a hand, stopping the Aedes in their tracks. "Please don't alarm our guests."

"Guests?" the first Aedes snarled.

Malcolm nodded. "Yes, Rob. These Davina are my guests."

"And you've shown them where we're hiding!" Rob yelled back.

Malcolm shook his head but replied calmly. "I already told you we've negotiated peace with a small group of Davina. These are the Davina seeking an alliance with us, and they've come to ask for our help."

"They're just kids!" someone shouted.

"Why would we help them?" someone else asked at the same time.

"QUIET!" Malcolm roared.

His voice was so commanding that I stumbled backward into Allie's feet. There was a reason these people respected him.

"Just listen to them," Malcolm instructed.

Malcolm looked to me, and I realized it was my turn to speak. I warily stepped forward, making sure to keep enough distance between myself and the closest Aedes in case anyone felt like attacking me.

"Look." My voice came out stronger than I felt. "I know you want to see the portal open. Malcolm told me that you'd like to return to Malum, but it's not possible."

Whispers traveled around the room.

"Shut it!" Malcolm snapped.

The church fell silent again.

"There's a reason the Davina closed the portals long ago," I explained. "It's because the realms are a threat to one another. If the portal opens all the way, the realms will collide. They'll destroy each other. It's why the Davina sealed off the portals in the first place."

"She's lying," someone accused.

"I don't think she is," Malcolm replied.

Several curious gazes met mine, but most Aedes narrowed their black eyes at me like they didn't believe me.

"The Davina no longer have the power to close the portal and protect our realm," I concluded. "We've come to ask if the Aedes have any ideas how to stop this."

"How would we know?" Rob snarled.

I tried to keep an even tone without snapping back at him. Now was *not* the time to get into an argument. "We thought maybe you'd heard stories that the Davina hadn't."

"Why should we listen to her?" a woman asked

Malcolm. "We should get to the portal and cross over to Malum as soon as possible!"

Echoes of agreement spread throughout the church.

"There's no guarantee you'd survive," I argued. "The realms could destroy each other before the portal opened enough to allow you to pass through. I know it's hard to view the earth as your home when you've been treated the way you have your whole life, but my hope is to help you make a home here if we survive this together."

"But you're a Davina," Rob pointed out. "Davina have never helped us before. Why should we trust you now?"

"I may be a—" I started, but several voices cut me off.

Soon, so many people were shouting that I couldn't make sense of what they were trying to say.

"SILENCE!" Malcolm roared, quieting the crowd once again.

I took a deep breath. "I may be a Davina, but I'm also human, and where I come from, we help each other out. I don't want to live in a world riddled with war and bloodshed any more than you do."

I expected an uproar again, but I was only met with silence. Rob's gaze turned to the ground. I waited… and waited.

"Please," Marek pleaded. "If anyone knows anything, now is the time to say something."

Someone cleared their throat at the other end of the church. All eyes fell upon the man. I stood on my toes to see him, but I couldn't get a good view from this distance.

"Ayden," Malcolm said, welcoming the man to come forward.

The crowd slowly parted until an old man reached the front. He stood slightly hunched, and his pale skin hung off his bones. He looked like he should be lying in a nursing home rather than fighting in this war.

Ayden's voice came out hoarse when he spoke. "I may have some information, but I don't know if it's true."

"Anything you might know can help us right now," I assured him.

The old man cleared his throat. "Long ago, there were rumors that the Aedes could unlock the powers of the Davina. It was said it was as if the gods themselves had been reincarnated. Perhaps there is truth to the rumor."

I glanced to Marek in uncertainty. This couldn't be the answer we were looking for, could it?

Marek caught my gaze then turned back to the old man. "Do the legends say how the Aedes do it?"

Ayden shook his head. "That is all the legend said. I do not know how they did it, only that somehow, the Aedes could make the Davina more powerful. As I said, I do not know if it is true. Our ancestors wouldn't have gone seeking the answer to making our enemies stronger."

I chewed my lower lip and thought about what he said. *Somehow, the Aedes could make the Davina more powerful.*

I was more powerful. And it only happened the first time when Malcolm fed off my essence.

I drew in an audible breath. "Malcolm, you did it once before."

His eyebrows drew together.

"Try it with me again," I demanded. "Feed off me."

"What?" Malcolm asked like I was insane.

"Feed off my essence, like you did before. I think that's the key."

Malcolm eyed me skeptically. "All that would do is unbalance your energies. It would weaken you."

"I insist," I told him.

Malcolm smirked and placed his hands on my shoulders. His eyes widened, and he inhaled a deep breath.

My skin chilled as fear overcame me. It was like I was in his house again, back to that moment when I thought this might be the end.

Then suddenly, a warm and comforting sensation consumed me. Essence tingled through my body, rising up from my toes and filling my heart. With each passing second, my body grew stronger. The essence inside of me felt as if a dam was opening, allowing me to pull magic from the earth and into my body.

It was as if Malcolm was helping to open the channel that my essence flowed through. I pictured that channel opening wider and wider, until I freely poured my essence into him. Malcolm's skin began to fill with color, and I could've sworn his lips seemed fuller. Even his dark irises seemed to dim to a more natural brown.

I turned my attention inward and focused on my essence. I channeled it from my heart and to my fingertips until white wisps of essence began flowing out of my palms. My essence crawled along the floor like fog.

The Aedes closest to us retreated several paces, and fear filled their eyes.

"Make her stop!" a woman cried.

I pulled the essence back to keep from scaring them and

let it fill the space around Malcolm and me. We locked eyes and exchanged a smile.

Malcolm's grip relaxed, and he turned to the crowd of Aedes. "It appears there is some truth to the rumors. Davina who share themselves with us grow stronger with us."

And yet, I wasn't sure this was enough. I wasn't sure *I* was enough.

"Let my friends try," I requested.

Marek and Casey looked eager to give it a shot, but Allie and Kyle shrank away in uncertainty.

"We need as much power as we can get to close the portal, and I need my friends' help," I said.

Malcolm nodded in agreement.

"I'll go first," Marek offered.

Rob was beside him a moment later. "I want to try."

Marek and Rob faced each other. I didn't know how Rob channeled essence from one person into himself. There were no visual cues apart from the look on both of their faces. I witnessed Marek shiver and knew he must've felt the chill rise to his skin. Then I saw the wonder in his eyes and knew he must be feeling that channel open wider.

Without warning, a fireball shot from his hand. It was a real fireball this time, with red flames and everything. I felt the heat cross my face as it shot across the room and slammed into the corner. A pile of dry leaves instantly caught fire. Flames licked into the air for a second before fizzling out to embers.

I heard Allie's audible intake of breath and Kyle's curse of surprise. Casey exhaled slowly, like she wanted to say something but couldn't find the words. Marek's eyes widened. He looked more shocked than the rest of us.

"What. Was. That?" Casey asked.

Marek held out his palm, and red flames rose into the air.

"Does it hurt?" I asked.

Marek shook his head. It looked like the flames should be burning the flesh off his bones, but his skin remained unharmed.

"Let us try," Allie said, intrigued to give it a shot.

Malcolm gestured for another three Aedes to come forward. He paired each of them with one of my friends. Allie shivered when the first Aedes accessed her essence. She held out her palm and narrowed her eyes in concentration. I expected a fireball or fog to rise out of her hand, but nothing came.

"Maybe it only works for some Davina," I thought out loud.

Allie's face fell in disappointment. Just as she dropped her hand, a gust of wind passed through the room.

Her eyes lit up. "Was that me? Did *I* do that?"

I couldn't find the words to respond. Had Allie just controlled *air*?

She concentrated and swiped her hand through the air again. Another gust of wind passed by me. Allie was shaping the air to her will.

Allie jumped up and down in excitement. "Let's see what Kyle can do!"

Casey and Kyle tried at the same time. Casey paired up with a tall, muscular Aedes with long dark hair, and her power manifested almost immediately. She willed the rock Marek had used into her hand. Slowly, dirt across the floor rose around us, as if someone had flipped off the switch to gravity. Casey had the power to control earth.

Kyle took the longest to discover what his essence was capable of. After trying to control fire, air, and earth, he'd almost given up. Outside, the clouds began to darken with his mood. When Allie pointed out the poor weather, Kyle rushed to the window.

"And then there was rain," he said just as the first of the raindrops hit the ground.

Within seconds, the rain pounding against the roof filled the room with a deafening roar. A moment later, it stopped.

"I don't get it," I thought out loud. "Why do we all have these different powers?"

The old man cleared his throat again. "It's like the stories said. The Aedes can unlock the power of the gods."

"It makes so much sense," Marek said. "These are all earth-creating powers like the gods had."

"How can we have this power in our mortal bodies if Grace's power was too much for me?" I asked.

Marek pressed his lips together, stumped.

"Maybe Grace's power was different because it wasn't *yours*," Kyle thought aloud. "Maybe it was working against you somehow because it still belonged to Grace."

Allie nodded, like she thought Kyle had a good point.

"We must've inherited the gods' powers all along," Marek theorized. "We just forgot how to access them on our own. Our ancestors, the Sanctities and Divinities, coexisted. Maybe this was one of the reasons the two races of gods worked together. Because together, they were stronger. Only with the help of the Aedes do the Davina have the power to access their full essence and become who they truly are."

Excitement sizzled in my bones. "And only with the Davina can the Aedes survive. They can feed off Davina essence without hurting anyone. This was how it was always meant to be! We can work together. The Davina can finally give back to the Aedes!"

Malcolm frowned. "Only if we can shut down the portal."

Well, shit. There was still that.

"We can do it together," I said with conviction. "Together, we should be able to generate enough power to collapse the portal and keep the realms from touching."

I turned back to the large group of Aedes still staring at me. "It's time for the Davina and the Aedes to put our differences aside and come together. If we survive this and the other Davina see what we can do together, then we can live in true peace once all this is over. I'm sorry for how they've treated you and that they've never listened to you before. It's time for that to change. I can't make up for the past, but perhaps we can change the future. I'm a Davina, and I'm here listening."

Murmurs spread across the room, and the Aedes exchanged glances with one another.

"The least we can do is try," I said. "Either we survive by working together, or we perish together."

A chilling silence fell over the chapel. Would we all be able to set aside our pride and give this a shot?

They're going to say no, I thought. *They'd rather die than help us.*

Dread spread throughout my body. Turning to the Aedes was our last option, and now we *would* die—all of us.

Ayden stepped forward on shaky feet. "I will follow Malcolm, whatever he decides."

"I will, too," a woman behind him agreed.

A chorus of agreement broke out across the church, raising my hopes.

I turned to Malcolm for confirmation. "You'll help us?"

He nodded once. "What do we have to do?"

I let out a shaky breath. "Follow me."

26

Hundreds of flapping wings followed behind me. I knew they were all Aedes, but the strange thing was that they sounded entirely Davina. Without looking back, I could imagine the group following behind me *were* Davina. We really weren't so different after all.

The clearing loomed up ahead. From this distance, the trees blocked my view of the ground, but I could see the rippling air of the portal rising above the tree line. Fear entered my chest. The portal had grown to massive proportions. I only hoped we weren't too late.

I passed above the outer edge of the clearing, and my fear quickly melted away. Instead, complete and utter hopelessness filled my body. The flapping of my wings faltered for a moment, and I dropped several feet before catching myself again.

Hundreds of Davina sat in the clearing facing the portal. I thought for sure we'd only have to fight off a few

Davina Council members, but this was a whole freaking army.

Good thing I brought my own army, I thought.

I heard the collective gasp below us as the Aedes following behind me swooped down into the clearing. Davina hurried to their feet. Essence shot from several people's hands before I had a chance to truly process my surprise.

I landed hard in the grass and raced forward toward the angry crowd of Davina. "STOP!"

"They've come in peace!" Marek shouted from beside me.

Davina hesitated when they spotted me and my friends at the front of the crowd. Several didn't seem to care and aimed more essence at the Aedes behind us. Black essence flew back in their direction.

Allie whirled around toward the Aedes. "No, wait! You have to show them you're better than this! We didn't come here to fight."

I opened my mouth to shout toward the Davina, to try to explain, but before I could say anything, a figure landed in front of me. I recognized Grace's large wings before I noticed her dark curls and white dress.

She faced the Davina and held her hands up. The chaos within the clearing calmed, leaving only the sound of rushing wind whipping through my hair. The burning smell had intensified and was so strong it made me want to hurl.

Grace slowly turned toward me. A hard expression settled on her face. "What are you doing, Ryn? You're ruining these last few moments the Davina have together."

"What are *you* doing here?" I couldn't help but let the accusation slip from my tongue before answering her. Was she *guarding* the portal from me?

Grace held her head high. "I thought it'd be best to wait out the end together."

"But it doesn't *have* to end," I argued. "The Aedes have agreed to help us."

Grace's lips turned down, and she eyed Malcolm beside me. "They can't help us. When are you going to accept that this is the end? There's nothing more you can do."

"But we can," I insisted. "The Aedes make us stronger. With their help, we can access more essence than we ever have before. We can collapse the portal!"

Davina exchanged glances with one another. Whispers spread across the clearing.

"You said it yourself, Grace," I pointed out. "You're not strong enough to do it on your own, but you're *not* alone. We can do this together. The Aedes and Davina are *meant* to be together."

Grace's features hardened. "I have no idea what you're talking about." The way she said it told me she was being honest.

"We'll show you," I offered.

I glanced to my friends. Together, we took a collective breath, and then all at once, we exposed our new powers. Fog lifted from my hand. Beside me, flames burst into the air out of Marek's palm. Kyle directed his hands toward the sky, and the clouds began to darken above him. Dirt rose from the ground in front of Casey and gathered into her hand. Allie produced a small whirlwind, causing the grass below her to blow out in all directions.

The entire crowd of Davina gasped and took a step back.

Even Grace stepped away from us. "What—?"

"Join our fight!" I called out above the wind. "Share yourself with the Aedes, and together, we can save our world!"

"NO!" Grace shouted. "This is insane! Ryn and her friends don't believe in our new world!"

"Nobody here will survive in your new world!" I spat. "You want to end the fighting, Grace. That doesn't start with genocide or whatever fresh start you're hoping for. It starts right here, with the Davina and the Aedes on the same side!"

Grace lowered her voice so only I could hear. "Just let it be, Ryn. The realms will die eventually, no matter what we do."

"They don't have to die *now* if we can prevent it," I argued.

"Ryn's a traitor!" Grace roared.

She looked out into the crowd of Davina, as if expecting them all to rush forward with murder in their eyes. They only stared back, unsure of who to follow.

"It won't hurt to let us try—" I started, but I was cut off when a white ball of energy whizzed between Marek and me.

The essence slammed into the Aedes behind me, knocking him out. His limp body fell into the Aedes beside him, and they caught him on his way to the ground. It took only a split second for my gaze to travel to the assailant. The essence had come from a young Davina boy who looked about fifteen. He stood there in shock, like he couldn't believe what he'd just done.

A moment later, chaos erupted in the clearing. Screams flew through the air, and Aedes and Davina rushed forward all around me until the two groups merged.

I instinctively ducked as essence rushed by my head. A strong hand gripped mine, pulling me back to my feet.

"Come on!" Marek shouted. "We have to get closer to the portal!"

I reached out for Allie, and we raced along behind Marek as he barreled his way through the crowd. I caught sight of Davina fighting Davina. One Davina took ahold of an Aedes's hand and shouted something in his ear. It looked like they were forming an alliance, but I was past them before I could see the outcome. Above us, Davina and Aedes flew through the sky. In only a matter of seconds, the two groups were evenly dispersed across the clearing, some of them fighting and others teaming up. It was impossible to tell who was on whose side.

My friends and I broke through the edge of the crowd just a few yards from the portal. Marek skidded to a halt, stopping so fast that I nearly rammed into him. I momentarily forgot about the fighting happening all around me as my eyes took in the portal in front of us.

It'd gone from being the size of a doorway to the size of a large house. The air rippled so violently that I couldn't make out the shapes swirling through it. I wasn't sure if I was looking beyond the portal to the trees anymore or if I was seeing Malum's landscape.

"Holy—" I started as I stared up at the grand feature in front of me.

Grace dropped down in front of me, blocking my view of the portal.

"Quick!" I shouted to Marek, Allie, and Kyle. Casey was nowhere to be seen. "Get as many people as close as you can to the portal—now!"

Kyle and Allie rushed away immediately to follow my orders.

"But I—" Marek started.

"I've got this!" I yelled at him.

"You never give up, do you?" Grace snarled.

I ignored her question. "It doesn't have to end like this."

Grace's lips curled into an evil, sardonic smile I'd never seen cross a Davina's face before. In that moment, it was clear that Grace would do whatever it took to hold me off until the world she'd come to despise was destroyed. My chance to convince her otherwise had long since passed. Grace had the power to end me in a heartbeat—and I could see in her eyes that she wanted to. I'd never be able to fight her.

"I need your help with Allie and Kyle!" I rose my voice at Marek.

Marek hesitated.

"Go!" I screamed. I wasn't going to let him stick around and watch me die.

Marek looked like it physically pained him to turn

away, but he did as I asked and rushed into the crowd to help round up people on our side.

Grace's hand twitched, and I knew instantly what was coming.

My death.

My life force would be severed right here at the foot of the portal.

No, I told myself. *I'm not going to die today.*

The thought passed through my mind in an instant. Grace's hand swung out. Just as purple electricity shot from her palm, I flinched away from her and threw my hands over my head like I was trying to protect myself from an avalanche.

Because that's totally going to help, Ryn, I told myself.

Shock hit me when I realized thoughts were still racing around in my head. I should've been knocked to my feet when Grace's essence hit me. It should've killed me. Grace was standing there ready to use her magic on me, and I had no time to get out of the way and no weapon to use against her.

Had she not attacked me?

I slowly peeled my eyes open and gasped. My foggy white essence had spread out from my hands and collided with Grace's crackling purple essence. It was like my essence acted as a shield against hers.

Well, Ryn. It looks like you were right. You're not going to die today.

I smiled at my inner voice.

My eyes met Grace's. A moment of confusion crossed her face, but it was instantly replaced by anger. The sounds of battle faded around me as I channeled essence into my palms.

"Not today, bitch," I muttered under my breath.

Essence exploded out of me, sending Grace's power back toward her. Grace flew off her feet and landed several yards away. I approached her with my newfound confidence. Essence snaked out of my hand and wrapped around her body. Grace dug her hands and feet into the ground and tried to distance herself from it, but it wrapped around her like a transparent rope, securing her arms to her sides. Her eyes widened.

I couldn't explain the strength that overcame me or how I knew what I was doing. All I knew was that I felt strong. *Damn* strong. And that I could use that strength to stop Grace. I guided my essence upward, pulling at Grace's body. Her feet dangled several inches above the ground.

"So this is what it's come to?" she choked out. "You're going to kill me?"

Her question hit me like a punch to the gut. I'd already killed too many times, but I couldn't let Grace get away with this. If I let her stop us, the end of the world was on my shoulders as well as hers.

"I'll do what I have to do," I stated in a strong voice. And I meant it.

Grace struggled to breathe. "You almost had me convinced."

My hold on her unexpectedly weakened, and I fought to squeeze tighter.

Grace shook her head, as if the whole thing amused her. "I was right all along. If teaming with the Aedes is the only way to stop this, it was never meant to be. Sooner or later, you will bring destruction down upon each other."

"You don't know that!" I shouted. The ground swayed beneath my feet, and I knew my energy was quickly draining.

"The gods lived in peace, and they destroyed each other," Grace pointed out.

"We're not the gods," I challenged. "We're different."

"You're right." Grace barely got the words out.

Without warning, purple electricity burst from the center of her chest. It spanned the air above me, crackling just inches above my head. My essence fizzled away, and Grace dropped to her feet. The drain of energy had disoriented me just long enough for Grace to gain her composure.

"You're nothing like the gods," Grace said a moment before her fist connected with my jaw.

Pain shot through my face, and I stumbled backward. The taste of copper filled my mouth.

What the hell? For a lady who'd spent thousands of years sleeping, you'd think her muscles would've atrophied, but Grace was *strong*.

I immediately shot a white fireball in Grace's direction, but my eyes were beginning to blur from the exertion. I missed completely.

Grace's hands were on me a moment later, gripping my shirt. "*I'm* the closest thing to a god now, and your weak essence can't defeat me."

Grace whipped me around and held my face just inches from the portal.

"NO!" I shrieked. I had no idea what would happen to me if she pushed me into the rippling air. I didn't want to find out.

Grace only laughed and yanked my body back. I landed hard on the ground several feet away. I gasped for the air that had been knocked from my chest and pushed myself onto my elbows.

My shoulders shook, but I forced my voice to remain strong. "Why do you care so much that you take everyone down with you?"

Grace didn't answer. Instead, she stared down at me with a smirk. Purple energy pulsed down her arm, and she readied herself to throw it at me—to end me.

I threw my hands in front of me again to block her attack. Tension built in my muscles as I fought to direct essence out of my body and toward her. Every inch of my body ached, as if I'd just run a marathon without any prior training. The essence I expected to shield me never came.

Grace raised her hands, and in that moment, I knew this was it. I didn't have the energy left to save myself.

Just as the thought crossed my mind, the earth began to shake beneath me. I thought for a moment that I might be having some sort of seizure, that all the fight had drained me to the point where my body gave up, too.

But then I noticed the mix of confusion and fear on Grace's face. She felt the violent shaking as well as I did, and just like me, she had no idea what was happening.

A sound like thunder filled the clearing, but unlike thunder, it wasn't met with a moment of silence following the initial *crack*. It continued, filling my ears to the point of pain. I couldn't even hear the violent winds over the sound of canons coming from inside the earth.

Then, the sound didn't seem to matter anymore. One moment, I was watching the grass shake beneath us. The next, the earth split, forming a massive cavern just feet from me.

I scurried backward and tried to get to my feet, but every time my hands left the ground, the intense shaking of the earth knocked me down again. I dared to glance back. The cavern was expanding, growing wider and wider by the second. Grace had fallen to the ground on the other side, and she stared at it in horror.

The cavern stretched along the length of the clearing and stopped at the portal. I drew in a sharp breath when I looked up to see what the portal had become. The air was no longer rippling in the center. Instead, a massive image of a new landscape formed. It was as if someone had punched a hole straight through the air. Dry, cracked sand and dark skies stretched as far as the eye could see.

Sheer terror ripped through my body.

This was Malum. And it was going to destroy us.

27

Grace's eyes darted to the portal, then back to me. Fear melted from her face, and a calm expression took over. It was the look of someone who'd found their peace.

"Marek!" I screamed, but I could hardly hear my own voice over the sound of the earth shattering around me.

His eyes met mine through the crowd. He raced toward me, pushing past people to get to me as fast as he could.

"We have to finish this. Now!" I shouted.

Marek reached me and pulled me to my feet. We stumbled as the earth continued rumbling beneath us, but I managed to stay upright without his support.

"We have to throw everything we've got into the portal," I instructed.

Allie and Kyle stumbled forward, trying to stay on two feet as they made their way toward us. Casey dropped out of the sky and landed next to me.

"Now!" I shouted.

Red flames shot from Marek's hands and into the portal, while Casey concentrated on trying to steady the earth. Color drained from her face as she strained to help. Allie and Kyle reached us and immediately began using their powers on the portal. Kyle summoned the power of the weather, and lightning struck down in front of us. Allie pushed the wind coming from the portal backward, using its energy against itself.

Fletcher landed beside Allie and focused on the grass beneath us. It grew and shaped to his will, tangling into the portal.

I gritted my teeth and fought to direct my essence toward Malum. Wisps escaped my hands in bursts, but it was nothing compared to the essence I used before. I glanced behind me quickly. Hordes of Aedes and Davina flocked away from the portal, but others still fought like they had nothing left to lose.

"Malcolm!" I shrieked.

Essence shot out of his palm and hit a Davina in the chest. His eyes met mine.

"We need help!" I yelled.

Malcolm gestured to a group of Aedes nearby for them to follow him. Moments later, he was beside me.

"I'm running out of energy!" I shouted over the deafening noises around us. "We all are. We need to access more!"

All around me, Davina and Aedes paired up. I noticed Gabe and Mr. Harris among the willing Davina. Aedes shot dark essence at the portal, while Davina used their new powers.

"No! Stop!" Grace shouted.

Malcolm gestured to another group of Aedes, and they took flight and dove toward Grace. Her scream ripped through the air as two of them grabbed her arms and dragged her into the sky, away from the portal.

"Take my essence, Malcolm," I demanded. "There's only one way to do this, and that's together."

Malcolm held his chin up. He didn't look scared at all; he looked brave. He nodded once, and then his strong hands were on my shoulders, pointing me back in the direction of the portal.

A chill spread across my skin, and I knew he was channeling my essence into him. The more he drew it out, the wider I felt the channel open. My body stopped shaking despite the ground moving beneath my feet, and I sensed my strength slowly return.

Essence fell from my fingertips and drew toward the portal in a stream. All around me, powers grew. Marek's flaming fireballs turned to a stream of fire, as if there was some sort of fuel suspended in the air for him to burn through. Kyle's lightning bolts hit one after the other, sending thunder echoing throughout the clearing. Aedes essence continued to shoot into the portal.

But all our essence did was distort the image of the landscape on the other side. The ground continued to shake, and the portal continued to widen.

"It's not working!" Marek shouted.

I can see that! I wanted to yell back, but I couldn't break my concentration.

My essence hit the portal and expanded inside of it,

swirling as if it'd hit a wall. Every muscle inside my body tensed as I willed it to do something… *anything*. I bit down on my lower lip until I tasted blood.

Why wasn't this working? We were collectively stronger than Grace, weren't we? Surely, together we had more power than the sixteen Originals had when they'd destroyed the portals the last time.

Maybe the portals weren't this strong.

Maybe they did something different.

Doubts raced through my mind. Any moment now, the earth would crack in half and destroy us all.

Aedes essence crossed my path, slamming into my stream of magic. My essence flickered from white to black and then back to white again. An electric tingle traveled along my skin.

A sharp breath passed my lips as a moment of clarity struck.

The only way to do this is together, I reminded myself.

Though we were working together as allies, we weren't working together as *one*. And that was the only way we'd survive.

I was the answer. I was the only one who could bring these people together. I had the power in me all along.

I pulled my essence from the portal and directed it into a large globe above us. My foggy essence spread out like a force field, and it only continued to grow.

"Stop aiming at the portal!" I instructed as loud as I could. "Fire at my essence instead!"

A confused expression crossed Marek's face, but he didn't waste a moment to comply. He shot his fire into the opening I'd left for him. It bounced around inside the giant orb, unable to escape.

Several people down the line took notice and followed suit. Soon, everyone was sending essence into one concentrated area. Fire, wind, lightning, and more whirled together. My force field expanded to the size of the school as power grew and sizzled inside of it. It was hundreds of times stronger and more electric than I'd ever felt from Grace's power.

I sealed off the force field, locking the collective magic inside of it. And then I squeezed, pulling all that magic together. The massive, powerful globe hovering above us glowed every color of the rainbow as the various types of essence bounced around inside, struggling to escape, begging to explode.

And they would… together.

A piercing cry ripped out of my lungs as I aimed my essence at the portal. It took everything I had to manipulate it, so much that I thought the exertion might tear me apart. A moment later, I felt the tethers of my magic break away from me.

And then came the blinding light and the deafening *boom* of a crumbling realm.

My ears were ringing. Why were my ears ringing? I should be dead. Ears don't ring when you're dead.

"Ryn!"

That voice. That beautiful angel's voice…

Angels didn't exist in death. What was one doing here?

"Ryn! Oh, shit. Please don't be dead."

I hate to break it to you...

"Marek," another voice said softly.

Marek?

Suddenly, everything that had happened to me since moving to Eagle Valley came rushing back in a blur, everything right up to that last moment, when our realm collapsed.

I blinked my eyes open. Warm sunlight caressed my face, almost blinding me.

"She's okay!" a female voice shrieked.

A strong force wrapped around my body and squeezed me tight. I struggled to breathe. The faint scent of leather hit my nose. It was so familiar. It was...

"Marek!" I cried as my eyes finally focused.

He pulled me into him tighter, burying his face into my tangled hair. He drew away from me only to place kiss after kiss on my lips. "I thought I'd lost you, but you're okay! You're okay!"

I finally had a chance to look around. Allie, Kyle, Casey, Malcolm, and Fletcher stood in a circle, surrounding me. Beyond them spanned a stretch of thick grass, and then a forest of trees. We were still in the clearing, but the roar of the wind and the shaking of the earth were gone. The large cavern remained, like a scar carved into the earth, but the portal was nowhere to be seen.

"What happened?" I asked.

"It worked!" Allie cried in excitement. "Your plan worked, Ryn. We collapsed the portal!"

"So, we're safe?" I asked, barely able to believe it. "And the war?"

Fletcher and Malcolm exchanged a glance.

"I think it's time we declare this war officially over," Fletcher said.

"Yes," Malcolm agreed. "I think it's finally time peace is restored."

Those words meant everything to me.

Malcolm reached out and pulled me to my feet. I was still trying to wrap my head around what we'd accomplished together. All this time, the Aedes and Davina had the power to work together as one.

This, I realized, was our divine fate.

EPILOGUE

*H*appiness filled me on our first day back at school over a week later. Aedes and Davina alike roamed the halls after class. The school was almost crowded now that Aedes were allowed to attend with us, but it was crowded in a good way, like we were all attending an amazing party together. New class schedules had been issued, and we were now training alongside the Aedes and learning how to harness our powers together.

I turned down a secluded hallway and gently knocked on Mrs. Presley's old office door.

"Come in," a male voice called from behind it.

I pushed the door open. Mr. Harris sat behind the large desk near the window, and Malcolm sat in one of the chairs across from him.

Malcolm stood when I entered the room. Color filled his skin, and his black irises had faded to brown. It was as if only Davina essence could restore the Aedes' health. Malcolm wore navy blue pants and a white button-down shirt. It was strange to see him in regular clothes and looking so… human.

No one knew exactly what happened when we destroyed the portal, but ever since then, the Aedes have been able to interact with our world. Fletcher theorized that when we destroyed the portal, we also destroyed Malum. He believed that their second curse—the one that kept them from fully existing here and from the humans being able to see them—was somehow tied to their realm and that when we destroyed it, we broke their curse. Somehow, their first curse remained, the one that marked them with darkness and made their feathery wings black and their essence dark.

Luckily, there were already Davina in government positions, which made assimilating the Aedes into our society easier than I would've thought.

"You wanted to see me?" I asked.

Mr. Harris leaned forward in his chair. "Let me start by apologizing."

I took a seat beside Malcolm. "You don't have to do that."

"I do," Mr. Harris said. "On behalf of the entire Davina Council, I hope you will find it in your heart to forgive us. As you may know, Anthony Lucas has resigned as the head of the Davina Council, and I've been voted in to take his place. However, we have decided to dissolve the Davina Council altogether. A new alliance is forming, and we're inviting members of all races to be a part of it."

He smiled cheerfully. "We cannot reveal ourselves to the entire population until a treaty is established. Naturally, humans are a bit wary of us. Our new alliance will need somebody to bring us all together and facilitate peace among our three races. We would like to offer you a position serving as a spokesperson for the alliance."

I glanced between Mr. Harris and Malcolm speechlessly. Was this some sort of joke?

I was surprised to find them both smiling back at me. They meant it. They wanted me to be their leader.

"Isn't that your job?" I asked Mr. Harris.

He smiled. "Yes, but we believe that you would serve us better in that role. The Davina and the Aedes found peace through you, and the humans need someone to listen to."

I shook my head. "Peace didn't come from me. It came from inside all of you. It was there all along. I just helped you realize it was possible."

"See?" Malcolm said. "That's why we need you."

I should've been jumping for joy at the offer, but I couldn't see myself in the position they saw me in. I was just a teenage girl trying to survive high school.

"I'm sorry," I said, "but I think I'm going have to respectfully decline. Politics aren't my thing."

Mr. Harris looked disappointed, but he nodded in understanding. He stood and reached his hand out. "Please let us know if you change your mind."

I shook his hand. "I will."

Malcolm crossed the room with me and smiled wide when he swung the door open. I never realized how much I took the simple act of opening a door for granted. Malcolm's whole life, he'd watched other people open doors but could never do it himself. It was strange how destroying the Aedes' chance at a true home had created a home for them here.

Malcolm followed me out of the office. "Do you mind if I have a word with you, Ryn?"

"Sure." I stopped in the middle of the hall.

He waited for a freshman to pass by us before speaking again. "I just wanted to know..."

I held my breath. I could already tell I wasn't going to like his question.

"Did he suffer?"

I thought I might vomit in response to those three words, but I managed to swallow down the lump in my throat and keep my lunch where it belonged. "Malcolm... I—"

"I'm not trying to blame you again," he interrupted. "I understand that you were only protecting yourself. I know now that Trenton made a sacrifice to create a new and better world. I just want to know if his sacrifice was... I want to know if..."

I wasn't sure Malcolm knew what he wanted, but I knew I could help him find his own peace.

"Malcolm," I interrupted.

His eyes lit up hopefully.

"He didn't feel a thing."

Malcolm relaxed, and then he reached out his hand. "Thank you."

I took his hand in mine and shook it. "I hope our new world ends up being everything you hoped for."

❧

"Where have you been?" Kyle asked once I reached the common room. He sat on one of the big cushy chairs in front of the fireplace.

Allie sat on his lap with her head rested against his shoulder. Marek had his legs draped over the armrest of the chair next to them.

"Hey," Casey's voice came casually before I could answer Kyle. "Long time, no see."

She sat on the couch beside an Aedes guy with dark eyes and long black hair. He had a muscular arm wrapped around her and a smug expression fixed on his face. I recognized him as the guy who first paired up with Casey in the church.

"Yeah," I said like we were old friends. "What have you been up to?"

"Oh, you know." She shrugged and glanced to Mr. Tall Dark and Handsome. "Making new friends."

Kyle scoffed and muttered under his breath, "Is that all?"

"Hey," Casey snapped the same time her boyfriend's jaw tightened. "I didn't ask your opinion."

"It's called free speech, Harris," Kyle said with an eye roll while Allie lightly elbowed him in the chest.

Some things never change, I thought.

"Anyway..." Casey turned back to me. "I never got to tell you that what you did was pretty awesome."

I couldn't help but smile. "Thanks. You were great, too."

"Of course I was," Casey teased. "I wouldn't have it any other way."

"No, you wouldn't," I replied with a laugh.

Casey beamed.

I turned to my friends. "Ready to go?"

Marek stood and laced his fingers in mine.

"Racing?" Allie asked in excitement.

Marek smirked. "What else?"

Allie hopped to her feet, and Kyle followed.

"Have fun," Casey called over her shoulder. I wasn't sure how much she meant it, but I appreciated the gesture.

We exited the back doors of the school. A figure in the distance caught my eye, and I paused.

"What?" Marek followed my gaze toward Grace, who sat in the grass across the lawn.

I dropped Marek's hand. "I need a minute."

He hesitated.

"I'll be fine," I promised. "Go have fun. I'll meet up with you soon."

Marek caught up with Allie and Kyle while I approached Grace. Her eyes were closed, and she inhaled deep breaths. I could tell she noticed my approach, because her eyelids flickered slightly, like I'd disrupted her concentration.

"Mind if I sit?" I asked.

Grace shook her head.

I lowered myself beside her. "How are you doing?"

She finally peeled her eyes open, but she ignored my question. "I'm sorry for all the trouble I caused."

I wasn't sure what to say, but Grace didn't give me a chance to respond before she spoke again.

"I don't just mean I'm sorry for not trying hard enough to save this world. I mean…" Her voice trailed off.

"What?" I asked curiously.

Grace met my gaze. "I'm sorry for letting the Council hurt your friend. You should know that I was the one who followed you to Malcolm's."

I inhaled an audible breath.

Grace's eyes dropped back to the grass. "I'm sorry I didn't believe you, Ryn. I didn't think that the Davina and the Aedes could truly come together. I didn't believe any of us deserved this world, but you have shown me that I was wrong."

I noticed her hands shaking, as if this was incredibly difficult for her to admit.

She swallowed hard. "You were right. Peace is possible."

I was amazed to hear the words come out of her mouth.

"There are more people out there who need convincing," I said. "Will you help us unify them?"

Grace shook her head. "My reputation has already been ruined. I think that job is best left to you."

I smiled shyly. "Mr. Harris already asked for my help, but I turned him down."

"Why?" Grace looked surprised.

I shrugged. "I'm not a leader. And let's face it, I don't know enough about the Davina to lead them. I have to stay here at Galen and graduate."

She nodded like she understood.

A silent beat passed between us, and I dared to break it. "So, if you're not going to help the Davina, what will you do now?"

Grace hesitated. "I'm leaving, Ryn."

My brow furrowed. "Where will you go?"

She took a long breath. "I'm going to join my family."

"But your family… Grace, you're talking about death."

"I've already made my decision," she said. "The Davina and the Aedes are strong enough together without me. There's no place for me in this world anymore."

"But, you're immortal," I pointed out.

"I will never die of old age," Grace explained, "but that doesn't mean my body can't be destroyed and my life force severed. I've already talked with Fletcher, and he is willing to help me find my peace."

"What?" I asked breathlessly. "How?"

"I will not bore you with the details," Grace answered. "My tomb will be moved from your house and placed inside Galen High. Tonight, I will enter an eternal slumber, and this time, I won't ever wake up."

Oh, wow. What was I supposed to say to that? Rest in peace?

"I'm sorry about how I treated you," I said instead. "I know you were only doing what you thought was best."

"Yes, but your way was better," Grace admitted. "I failed as a leader. You will be the Davina's new hope now."

I looked toward the line of trees that met up with the lawn, contemplating her words. "I don't know if I want people to look up to me."

Grace breathed a heavy sigh. "I made a lot of mistakes, but I think the one thing I did right was choosing you. You didn't need to wake me to make the difference."

"But I did," I argued. "You pushed me in the right direction. We wouldn't be here without you."

Grace smiled. Silence passed between us once again,

but finally, she turned to me. "Before I leave, I'd like to do one thing right."

My curiosity piqued. "What's that?"

"I'd like to leave you with a piece of advice. You say you don't want people looking up to you, but they will. Be careful what you say and do, Ryn. Someone will always be watching, and they'll be searching for inspiration. So please, keep doing what you're doing, and *inspire* them."

My jaw went slack as I tried to come up with the right words. It was strange to think that so many people would look up to me, but I couldn't deny that this was my destiny, whether I wanted it or not.

I held my head high. "I'll do my best."

Grace nodded. "I know you will."

It seemed like several minutes passed before I spoke again. "Do you want me to stay with you until...?"

Grace shook her head. "No. I know my peace is coming. I don't need any more comfort than that."

I thought, for a moment, she was only saying that to spare me the trouble, but she looked like she meant it. Grace had finally found her peace.

Once Grace said goodbye, I headed down the trail toward the valley. The bright sunlight filtered in through the leaves above my head, casting dancing rays along the forest floor. It was so beautiful that I couldn't believe these woods had once scared me.

I broke out of the trees to see black and white wings all throughout the valley. The last time I saw something like this, we were trying to kill each other. Now the Aedes and Davina were becoming friends.

I jumped back in surprise as Allie streaked past me. She raced laps around the valley with her wings spread wide. Marek flew by behind her a second later, followed by Kyle.

A wide smile spread across my face. I flexed my shoulders and jumped into the air to follow behind them. For the first time since discovering what I was, I felt like a normal Davina.

~

The day grew long as more Aedes and Davina joined us in the valley. I lay on my back in the grass with my wings spread out beneath me, staring up at the pink sky.

"Hey."

My heart flipped at the sound of Marek's voice. I turned my head to see him approaching. He knelt to one knee beside me and held his hand out.

"Come on," he encouraged. "What do you say about one last flight?"

I let my head fall back to the comfortable grass. "No, that's okay. I'm exhausted anyway."

A smile crept across his face. "I'm not asking you to race me. I'm asking you to follow me."

I didn't ask any further questions. I took his hand, and Marek pulled me to my feet. The wind whipped through my hair a moment later as I followed along through the sky beside him.

We landed at the top of the rocky hill outside of town —*our hill*. Marek pulled his wings into him and sat on the ground overlooking town. I joined him and snuggled into his bare chest.

Marek placed a kiss on the top of my head. "I love you, Ryn."

My heart fluttered at the sound of those magical words. "I know, Marek. I love you, too."

He reached out to touch my chin and pull my gaze to his. "You saved me, you know."

I saved him?

"From what?" I asked.

"From myself," Marek replied. "I see the world differently now, and it's all because of you."

A smile crept across my face. "I hope that's a good thing."

Marek laughed lightly. "Of course it is."

I snuggled back into him and inhaled his soothing scent. We stared out at the sunset for several minutes before Marek spoke again.

"Ryn? How do you feel, now that things are over?"

How do I even begin to answer that question?

I took a deep breath before speaking. "I feel… at peace."

"Even after what happened with Trenton?" Marek asked.

I carefully considered the question. I still wished I could take back what I did, but I knew wishing for such a thing was futile.

"Yeah," I answered honestly. "The Aedes have finally found their home. I think that if Trenton were here, he'd be smiling for them."

Marek nodded. "I think so, too."

My gaze dropped to the feather around his neck. "Marek, what do you think will happen next? With us, I mean."

Marek shrugged, but he looked deep in thought. "We'll graduate…"

"And then what?"

He returned his gaze to the landscape in front of us. "I still want to protect, like always."

"But the war is over," I pointed out. "There's nothing to protect *from*."

Marek breathed a heavy sigh. "We won *this* war. But there are many other battles to be fought."

"Does that mean you're going into the armed forces?" I asked.

Marek paused, as if considering the idea. He rested his head on mine before answering. "I was thinking law enforcement, like becoming a police officer."

I was so relaxed in his arms that my voice fell to a soft whisper. "That sounds perfect."

Marek trailed his fingers across the back of my hand, sending shivers up and down my spine. "What about you? Where do you want to go after graduation?"

I thought about the question for several moments. What *did* I want?

I laced my fingers through his. "I think I'd still like to become a chef. I could open my own restaurant. I don't want to be a part of the fighting anymore. I just want to live a quiet, normal life raising kids and baking cookies."

"Mm… cookies," Marek responded with a smile.

I beamed back at him. "I'll make you cookies anytime

you want. No matter what happens, I'll follow you anywhere."

Marek squeezed me tightly, like those were the exact words he'd hoped to hear. "Are you ready to face our future together?"

"Yes," I said without hesitation. "Because I know that no matter what, we'll be together."

I barely finished the sentence before Marek's lips were on mine, sending a surge of passion throughout my body.

For the first time in my life, everything was absolutely perfect.

END OF BOOK THREE

The Davina return in book one of the Divine Descendants Duology, *Concealing Magic*.

ABOUT THE AUTHOR

Alicia Rades is a USA Today bestselling author of young adult and new adult paranormal fiction. When she's not dreaming up magical stories, she's either binge-watching paranormal TV shows, meditating, or spending time with her family. She has an unhealthy obsession with psychic characters and writes with a deck of tarot cards next to her computer.